Martha pushed Jonathan into the door. She could hear muffled banging and bumping coming from the weather house. Then she saw Mr Tom emerge from the house, looking a little ruffled. He stepped down from the large book on which the house had been placed and caught sight of Jonathan and Martha.

"Good day to you," he said, flourishing his hat politely.

"It's the weather people – they've come alive," said Martha quickly to Jonathan before he had time to take his first surprised breath. "They'll give me wishes and I want you to share the first one. What shall we do? Come on, think. Lots of money? Flying? Invisible? Let's have it now, right away, before anybody wakes up!"

NINA BEACHCROFT

The Wishing People

MAMMOTH

First published in Great Britain 1980
by William Heinemann Ltd
Published 1992 by Mammoth
an imprint of Mandarin Paperbacks
Michelin House, 81 Fulham Road, London SW3 6RB

Mandarin is an imprint of the Octopus Publishing Group,
a division of Reed International Books Ltd

Copyright © Nina Beachcroft 1980

ISBN 0 7497 0940 5

A CIP catalogue record for this title
is available from the British Library

Printed in Great Britain
by Cox & Wyman Ltd, Reading, Berkshire

1

They were obviously a husband and wife. He stood a pace or
two outside his door, his hat in his hand, and a look of cheerful
good humour on his face. She was withdrawn a little way
inside her door (there were two open doors to their house) and
she had an umbrella up over her head, though she could not
possibly need it, standing within the door as she did. Her face
was rather solemn, severe even; her hair scraped back from
her head into a neat bun.

Martha fell in love with them at once and wanted to own
them. She wanted to repaint their house for them which had
once been green and white; she wanted the weather to change
and to see the woman with her umbrella emerging.

'Do you think it works?' she asked her mother more than
once. 'It's a fine day now and the man *is* outside. Do you think
if it began to rain we'd see her move? How on earth does it
work? I want to see it work. How much is it going to fetch? I'd
love to have it in my room.'

'I wonder what it's worth,' Martha's mother walked up to
the little green and white house. 'It could well reach a fancy
price like so many of those old-fashioned things. It looks early
Victorian to me.'

'Please will you bid for it?' begged Martha. 'It's my
birthday next week. If you haven't got me anything yet, please
may I have that?'

'What a funny thing to choose,' said her mother a little
doubtfully. 'We'll see how soon it comes up, then, and if they
throw it in with anything else. I don't want to sit here all day.
I really only wanted to wait for those three Windsor chairs.
They are lot 27. I'd better get a catalogue: what's the number
of the weather house?'

'Fifty-one,' said Martha, examining the back of the house.

Her mother made a doubtful face. 'Well . . .' she said, and then, 'Oh look, there's Jonathan and his mother. *And* the Robertsons. Everybody's coming to this sale. Sheer curiosity to see what was in the old man's house, of course. It's not as if he was a great antique collector or had much taste.'

'I think he had some lovely things,' said Martha, looking round her at the great mass of objects: china, glass, chairs, tables, pictures and clocks, all arrayed in the various big rooms of the house where two months ago old Mr Wormly had died. His relations hadn't taken anything because he'd only had a nephew in Canada. And so the contents of his house were being auctioned off. This was the preview and at eleven o'clock precisely the sale would begin.

Meanwhile Martha's mother was greeting Jonathan's mother. 'Hullo, Irene,' she said in the polite, rather reserved voice she kept for Jonathan's mother, whom she didn't like. 'Is there anything special that attracts you here?'

'Not really, Ruth,' said Jonathan's mother in her usual rather plaintive voice. She didn't like Martha's mother either, at least Martha was pretty sure she didn't. 'It's an extraordinary collection of junk, isn't it? Apparently the old man got very eccentric and went about buying all sorts of things he didn't need.'

'I'm bored,' said Jonathan in Martha's ear. 'Let's explore on our own.'

'All right.'

So they pushed their way between crowds of neighbours and villagers, all of whom were chatting away as if they hadn't seen one another in months. In the large panelled hall of the old house there were many more interesting things; a sword in its scabbard, enormous garden urns, a dusty billiard table with a broken leg, and a full-length cracked and dirty mirror propped up against a wall.

'Look!' cried Jonathan in delight. 'It changes you.'

His huge head loomed in the mirror; misshapen, as large again as his body.

'Strange,' said Martha, waving at it. Now her hand was

6

small, now large. 'Do you think Mr Wormly used to do this?' She walked nearer the mirror, watching herself grow.

'Fancy being a giant,' she said. 'Or very small. Oh, Jonathan, there's a little house, so sweet – '

But Jonathan wasn't listening. He continued to posture before the mirror. It made him look incredibly ugly, and in fact he was quite a good looking boy, fair and neat, and very unlike Martha, who was small, dark and untidy, and jumped about a lot in an excitable manner.

Martha decided to leave Jonathan and find her mother again. She could see him any old time, he lived next door. They saw quite a lot of one another, because none of the other children from the village school lived up their way, and Jonathan, being an only child, needed company.

In what had been the dining-room of the house, Martha came upon her older sister Anna, standing under a picture of Highland cattle, lot 42. Her shaggy hair was not unlike theirs. She only needed a pair of sharp horns.

'Just looking round,' said Anna vaguely, darting a very keen look after a young man of about twenty who had just pushed past.

'Anna, if Mummy won't, will you bid for the little weather house for me, please? It's lot 51 and it can be your birthday present to me,' said Martha hopefully.

'I haven't that sort of money to spare,' said Anna with one of her withering looks.

Martha thought for a moment of appealing to the two brothers who came between herself and Anna in age, but then remembered that neither Paul nor Mark were likely to have come to the auction. Nor did they ever have any money to spare, either.

Outside the front door of the house, standing on the gravelled drive, Martha found her father, talking to another man very loudly and heartily. She didn't like to interrupt them, so had to wait listening to lots of boring talk about the new village hall, until she had an opportunity to pull at her father's arm and beg him, 'Dear nice Daddy, will you get the little weather house for me – it shouldn't cost much.'

'What weather house? Oh, you mean one of those barometer things . . . I wasn't meaning to stay long, you know.
Just taking a look at the pictures – as much for the frames as
for anything else – never know when one mightn't pick up a
good frame . . .'

'Come *on*, Martha,' said Jonathan, suddenly appearing at
her side.

'Coming,' Martha abandoned her idea of owning the
weather house. She had the most unobliging family in the
world, she knew that for sure. Intent only on their own
interests, they had little time to spread joy around them by
unselfish giving . . . It wasn't as if she were asking for much.
Only a little wooden house with a man and wife who came in
and out according to the weather.

'And I didn't get the chairs,' exclaimed Martha's mother
coming into their house sometime in the late afternoon. 'I
found myself bidding against Mr Feather from The Bull and
the price ran up too high for me. I'm dying for a cup of tea.
Oh – yes – Martha, the house you wanted is in the boot of the
car. I had to buy a rusty coal scuttle which I don't want which
went with it . . . Oh well. The auctioneer wasn't sure the
barometer was working too well so I got it cheaply. You can
have something else for your birthday to go with it.'

'Thank you very much,' cried Martha in surprise. She had
spent the afternoon with Jonathan and quite forgotten the
house and the little husband and wife. So she fetched them
from the boot of the car and got a wet rag and wiped off the
dust and cobwebs and decided whereabouts in her room to
put them. Sometimes such houses were fixed to the wall but
this had no way of fitting on and she decided to put it for the
time being on her window sill. The sun was still out and it was
warm and she fancied that the man had come a little further
out. He looked jolly; whoever had carved him out of wood had
given him rough curly hair and had painted his cheeks with
two red spots. His mouth was smiling. Now she could examine
the house at her leisure, she could see that there was a window
with red curtains painted on one side of it and the roof had low

8

eaves and a chimney pot. It was a cottage sort of house. Then she found another little window, high up under the eaves as if the cottage had an upstairs, though in fact it didn't; there was nothing inside except the mechanism which worked the man and woman in and out through their doors.

'I'll buy you some paint for your birthday to paint it up a bit,' offered Anna, who had drifted into Martha's room for a minute, and was examining her face in Martha's mirror.

'Yes, *please*,' said Martha quickly. 'It would be nice to smarten the cottage up.' Perhaps she could do something to the little people. They were about two inches high. The man had a faded blue jacket on which reached quite far down his legs and what looked like grey and blue trousers beneath. The woman had simply a long blue dress which came nearly to her feet; you could just see little black boots sticking out below. And she was holding a black umbrella over her head. Her face looked as if it had been forgotten, because it was just pale wood colour, no red to her cheeks, and she wasn't smiling.

She looked rather sad and cross, as was fitting for someone who could only come out when it was raining.

'That's *my* pencil sharpener,' said Anna suddenly, pouncing. 'Honestly, Martha, why can't you keep out of my room? You're not to *have* my things.'

Martha was about to defend herself hotly, although she had no real defence, when she remembered about the promise of paint.

'Sorry,' she said meekly. 'I only needed to sharpen a pencil . . .'

'Buy your own pencil sharpeners,' continued Anna.

'How can I when I have hardly any money and I can't get to shops much!' shouted Martha, but Anna had gone.

Martha sighed deeply, feeling life was unfair to her, as she so often did. It was wretched being the youngest. She was the only one still at primary school, the only one not allowed to take the bus on her own into town and shop properly, instead of at the one village shop which had nothing worth buying anyway, the only one not allowed to watch television as long as she liked in the evening – the only one –

'Supper time!' her father bellowed up the stairs, and Martha forgot her grievances, and the weather house, and ran downstairs.

2

Martha lay on her back fast asleep. Her mouth was partially open, but she was not snoring. She was, however, dreaming. In her dream she was talking to someone – people – in her room. The moon lit them up for her: they were the weatherman and his wife, full-size people, sitting in her room and talking to her about herself.

'I am Martha, and I'm the youngest,' Martha was saying . . . because her mouth was open she gave a sudden snort and woke herself up.

The moonlight was flooding in through the half-open curtains, full on to the weather house. It was bright enough for her to see a small difference; both man and wife now stood equally at their open doors, looking at her. But they were only small wooden figures.

Martha got out of bed, advanced into the moonlight, bathed in it, its white light lapping round her, covering her. She bent down to look at the weather people, the memory of the dream-conversation she had been having with them still strong within her.

'I wish you were alive,' she said to them.

And then Martha sat down on the end of her bed, because something had made her lose her balance. She had the oddest rumbling, vibrating feeling for a moment, almost as if she had been in an earthquake. The air round her seemed to hum: to give off a thin silvery sound. And she heard a sneeze, a shrill, tiny sneeze, the kind of sneeze a mouse might give.

'Bless you my dear,' said a faint voice.

'Atishoo!' There was the sneeze again – then another, rather sharper voice, the same voice that had sneezed said: 'Tom! Tom! Do you realize what has happened?'

'Yes, oh my goodness, it's happened at last!'

'Come on, come on then, don't stare about you like a great ninny. Get a move on!'

Martha sat rigid with excitement, not daring to move. For it looked, it seemed, in the brilliant moonlight as if the impossible, her wish, had come true. There were the two little people sneezing, moving, stretching themselves, yawning, coughing, speaking to one another in tones which though small and faint, showed a growing strength – finally they clambered off the mechanism which had held them in place and walked to and fro, on the window sill, between the green curtains. The woman closed her umbrella with a distinct click, smoothed down her dress, the man blew into his hat, patted it into his hand and finally put it onto his head. Then he caught sight of Martha staring in trance-like wonder at him.

He walked to the edge of the window sill, and swept the hat off his head in a low bow to her.

'Good evening,' he said. 'Your very humble servant, my dear Madam.'

Martha couldn't say anything; she merely stared at him in open-mouthed wonder.

'Is that the child who wished?' cried the woman, bustling up to the edge of the sill to stand alongside her husband.

'It must be. We owe her a great debt,' said the man bowing again.

'Is she deaf and dumb then? Why doesn't she introduce herself?'

'I think she is a little astonished, my dear.'

'What's the point of that? Why make a wish and then be astonished when it comes true, there's not much sense in that. I hope we've not struck a fool.'

'Hush, my dear, remember her feelings – ' the man was beginning, but then the woman pointed her umbrella at Martha and said in a sharp, brisk, no-nonsense voice, 'Speak up, girl, if you can. Since we're going to spend a little time together, we'd better know your name.'

'My name is Martha – Martha Grant,' stammered Martha at last. 'Have you really come alive because of my wish?'

'It would seem so,' said the little woman, a shade drily. But then she added quickly, as if she wanted to get the words over and done with, 'I'm not one for being enthusiastic – you can leave that to my husband Tom (I'm Mrs Tom by the way) but I do want to say "thank you"; and I'm an honourable woman. I'm aware of my debt.'

'My dear,' put in her husband warmly to Martha. 'We are immensely grateful to you. Can we ever repay you? You have delivered us, for a time anyway, from the power of an enchanter, and we are eternally at your service.'

'No we're not!' cried Mrs Tom beside him, poking him with the umbrella. 'Don't *exaggerate*, Tom. We are *not* eternally at your service, Martha. But we will repay. How old are you, child?'

'How *old*?' said Martha bewildered. For a moment in her general amazement and shock she forgot how old she was –she was the youngest, she knew that, for some reason that stuck in her memory, but how many years . . . Then she came to herself. Of course. Her tenth birthday was next week. And she had had one of her presents already. There it was, on the mantelpiece, talking to her, as if it were the most natural thing in the world.

'I'm nine now. And ten next week,' she said. 'Next Tuesday.'

'We'll count it as if you were ten,' said Mrs Tom rapidly. 'And remember that you've already had one of them, when you wished us alive. So, Martha Grant, that makes nine more. Would you like to start now or wait until tomorrow morning?'

'Start what?' Martha asked in bewilderment.

'My goodness – the child *is* an idiot,' she heard the woman say impatiently, but she was hushed by her husband.

'Ssh, my dear. Remember how times have changed. We've been confined for a long time now. She may not have read the old tales. She may not even be able to read.'

'Of course I can read!' burst out Martha indignantly.

'Perhaps you've not read the tales about those released from enchantment, or perhaps you didn't believe them? But

13

they were true. You see, you can exact your due, just as they say. One for each year of your life.'

'You mean . . .' began Martha, a great surge of incredulous excitement beginning to rise within her, 'I can have nine – '

'Wishes, of course,' cut in Mrs Tom impatiently before Martha could finish her sentence.

'We owe you nine wishes and being honourable people we will grant them to the best of our ability.'

'To the best of our ability and with the greatest pleasure,' put in Tom, smiling at Martha.

'To the best of our ability – and as for pleasure – well, that depends.'

'So come on, Martha,' they both spoke together now. 'Do you want to begin? We are your servants, wet or fine, if the North wind blows or the South, come flood, fire or earthquake. We are stronger and cleverer than you know, so what is the first wish?'

'I don't know,' faltered Martha. A dozen ideas spun round in her head. 'I wish you'd given me a little time – No – I mean – I don't mean that to be a proper wish. I wish I – I would like to know more about what you can do. I realize you must be magic, marvellous people. But why were you enchanted and kept in that house in the first place?'

There was a silence. Martha had asked the question because she truly did want to know the answer but also to give herself a little time to think. Somewhere at the back of her mind she knew she had at least nine urgent wishes – but it was hard to think coherently and sensibly at this late hour, in the middle of the night.

The silence persisted. Mr and Mrs Tom looked at each other and cleared their throats. Finally Mrs Tom spoke: 'Not within the terms of the contract!' she said.

'You see, Martha,' her husband put in apologetically, 'We understand that you want to know. But when the *cause* of the enchantment does not reflect perfectly to our credit you must understand we have a natural embarrassment . . . suffice it to say – '

'It is sufficient to say we were bound together in our house, without the opportunity to meet properly – I mean when the one was *out* the other was *in* as you might say – until the time came when somebody should like us and wish us alive again just at the right time – '

'The moon had to be full,' put in Mr Tom.

'Yes, the moon had to be full, and thus, you see, Martha, it happened at last. But it has taken a long, long time. I knew it would happen eventually, of course.'

'Really,' he said turning to her. 'What were all the sighs and moans about, then? Now I; I put a good face on it.'

'Oh, Tom,' she was beginning impatiently when there was a noise outside Martha's door. Another door had opened and a light clicked on and they heard a footstep.

Instantly, Mr and Mrs Tom were back in their places in their house as if they had never moved.

'Are you all right, Martha?' came her mother's voice and the door opened slightly. 'I heard you talking away. Were you having a dream?'

'Yes!' called Martha, hastily snuggling down in bed.

'Go to sleep again. It's nearly one o'clock. Night Night.'

'Good night,' murmured Martha, suddenly immensely tired and she fell asleep as her mother softly closed the door, almost as if she had been enchanted herself.

Martha woke at dawn, when the birds were beginning to chirp and call. She heard a bantam cock crowing shrilly from the cottage over the road; she heard a far-off cuckoo. It was five o'clock: a beautiful morning at the end of May. She lay a moment wondering why she had awoken with such a feeling of excitement; then remembered and jumped out of bed.

The sky outside her window was pink and pearly, the rising sun gilded the weather house. But where were Tom and Mrs Tom? They weren't at the doors of their house, had they run away?

Martha barely had time to agonize over this because she caught sight of something white crammed into the back of her house. It looked like one of her socks. Peering into the house she could see Mr and Mrs Tom lying at the back on the sock which partially covered them, and had been made into a bed and quilt combined. They lay side by side on their backs, their mouths drooped open. As she stared at them they began to wake up.

'You were snoring,' she heard Mrs Tom say.

'I daresay I was. What of it?' he replied through a great yawn.

'What o'clock is it?'

'And what weather is it? The sky looks dark, oh no, it is a face, peering in at us. Good morning, Martha!' he called, rising from his bed and stretching. 'You see we bedded down warm and snug. Your sock was conveniently placed on the back of the chair. I could just reach it and haul it in with the handle of Mrs Tom's umbrella.'

'I'd have preferred a clean sock,' sniffed Mrs Tom, smoothing her hair. 'And it's very inconvenient having our house on this high window sill with no means of getting off it. The curtains are too short to slide down. We don't want to break our necks. So could you lift us down to the floor, immediately, Martha, please. And then, if we're to remain here for a while, I've a list of things I want you to do for me.'

'All right.' Martha lifted the house down as gently as she could to a running accompaniment of commands from Mrs Tom, clinging to her door.

'Don't tilt us. Over there – no, not *there*. There. By the bookcase. I would like the house to be a little off the ground – not too far. The carpet's too dusty, it will make me sneeze. Does nobody do any housework in your house? Your maid-servant must be a lazy one. You'd better put a book under our house, a good fat one – but not too thick. I don't want to have to step too far down.'

When at last Martha had arranged the house to Mrs Tom's satisfaction and provided her with some cotton wool and clean handkerchiefs for the bed and put on the sock together with other necessary garments, she heard the dining-room clock downstairs striking the half hour. It was still very early, far too early for any of her family to be stirring, especially as it was the half term holiday and nobody need go to school. The birds outside were deafening, and now she could hear the occasional early lorry driving down the road at the front of the house.

Looking out of her window, Martha could not only see her back garden, large and untidy with a good deal of uncut grass at the bottom of it and a few aged fruit trees, but she could see over into a portion of her friend Jonathan's garden. This garden was always spotless, without a weed. The only slightly untidy thing in it was Jonathan's rabbit hutch which housed his large and fierce buck rabbit, Hercules. Martha leaned right out of the window, because there, unexpectedly, *was* Jonathan, up very early, bearing cabbage leaves for Hercules.

'Psst!' called Martha.

'Eh?' It was funny to see him jump, and look the wrong way.

'Here, it's me. I've something terribly exciting to show you. Can you come round to our house? I'll go and unlock the door and let you in.'

'Oh – all right,' said the imperturbable Jonathan as if it were the most natural thing to be summoned so early in the morning.

As Martha let him in as softly as she could because she didn't want to wake her family, she had a moment's qualm. She had realized that she wanted to share the weather people with Jonathan – but would they mind? Would his entrance into her room turn them back into wood? When she spoke to Jonathan and left the room, Mr Tom was re-making the bed under his wife's instructions and they hadn't noticed what she was doing.

Martha pushed Jonathan into her room and shut the door. She could hear a muffled banging and bumping coming from the weather house.

'Drat!' she heard Mrs Tom's shrill tones. 'I've barked my shin on that blessed machinery. Tom – it's your fault. There's no room to *move* in here – you can just go and take yourself off.'

Then Martha saw Mr Tom emerge from the house, looking a little ruffled. He stepped down from the large book on which the house had been placed, and caught sight of Jonathan and Martha.

'Good day to you,' he said, flourishing his hat politely. He did not seem in the least put out to see Jonathan.

'It's the weather people – they've come alive,' said Martha

17

quickly to Jonathan before he had time to take his first surprised breath. 'They'll give me wishes and I want you to share the first one. What shall we do? Come on, think. Lots of money? Flying? Invisible? Let's have it now, right away, before anybody wakes up!'

Some time later Martha, carrying the weather house rather awkwardly under one arm, and Jonathan, carrying a basket very carefully by the handle, could have been seen if there was anybody about to see them trudging up the road together. In the basket, protected with tissue paper and moss from the rough sides, rode Mr and Mrs Tom. Both Mr and Mrs Tom had insisted on the weather house coming too.

'We daren't risk being caught without it,' they had said. 'Where we go, it goes. If you will choose a wish that has to take place two miles away, you've only yourself to blame.'

Neither Martha nor Jonathan wished to waste a wish on something so ordinary as moving two miles – hence the long walk.

They turned off the road (they had long ago left their village behind) and took a bridle path which would lead them up through the beechwoods to the bare grassy top of the hills. Up there was a different sort of country; lonely, peaceful, timeless.

It was the best place, Martha and Jonathan were agreed. They would have privacy; an essential thing for a first wish, when one is not quite sure how it will turn out.

His first incredulity over, Jonathan now took the weather people as matter of factly as Martha; one cannot be incredulous too long when one's arm aches from the strain of carefully carrying two people a long, long way in a basket, even if the people are an unusual size, and claim magic powers.

Mrs Tom criticized the way the basket was held and swung once or twice, but mostly she and Mr Tom stood, side by side, looking out over the basket's edge and breathing in the fresh air.

'Larks still making the same old din as ever,' said Mrs

Tom tartly as they finally emerged from the hushed, green woods to the grassy slopes beyond and saw the blue distances unfold themselves to mingle with the pale blue sky.

But Martha, looking at her, saw her suddenly brush her hand against her eye, as if to wipe it.

'Butterflies very fine this season,' said Mr Tom, pointing to several greenish gold scraps, the same colour as the new beech leaves, which were dancing over the turf before them.

'Hm – stupid things. Now I like an insect that's of use – bees, for instance. They have *something* in their heads, not much, I grant you, but something.'

'Shall we try it somewhere here?' asked Martha, her heart beating.

'Just as you like,' said Mrs Tom indifferently. 'You'd better put that house down on the turf, then. That's a good spot. Now then, Jonathan, or whatever your name is, boy, look lively. Put us down gently – *gently* mind.'

When the weather people had climbed out and walked a little way on the turf near their house, they proclaimed themselves ready. Mrs Tom unexpectedly produced a little notebook and stub of pencil from the pocket of her dress. 'To business,' she said. 'Wish number one of the nine we owe you. It has to be recorded and signed by one of us on completion. If there's anything unsatisfactory – to either party – it has to be clearly stated.'

Martha took a deep breath. 'I wish – *we* wish – we could fly,' she said.

Nothing happened. She and Jonathan still stood firmly, side by side on the grass.

'Come on, come on,' cried Mrs Tom impatiently, writing busily and then closing the notebook. 'Don't expect us to do *all* the work. You have to make some effort.'

'Try a little jump,' suggested Mr Tom mildly. 'See what happens then.'

So Martha and Jonathan jumped – not very high, but they must have been strangely light, for they hovered, cleared the tops of the high grasses, came down as gently as pieces of thistledown.

'This is OK,' shouted Jonathan, suddenly getting the hang of it. He jumped higher, and downhill, and this time floated off some distance, laughing with excitement. Martha leapt too, descended a little way, then found she could stay in the air, almost, if not quite as long as she wished. Her body was now incredibly light. She soared, and the earth fell away beneath her in a broad sunlit sweep of colour. She turned in mid air, and floated back to see the tiny figure of Mr Tom gaily waving his hat to her. Mrs Tom wasn't even looking at her, she was wandering amongst a jungle of flowers, some of them taller than she was.

The sun climbed a little higher, it grew warmer and still Martha and Jonathan floated and descended and jumped again and again. It was not like being a bird – they couldn't use their arms as wings – and every now and then they gently descended whether they meant to or no, and had to jump off again.

'It's like being weightless in space,' said Jonathan as he soared past Martha. 'It's like that book about the moon, only they didn't have space suits in it because it was written too early – by that man – can't remember his name – '

'What?' called Martha, who hadn't read it.

'H. G. Wells!' he cried, as he floated past her.

'Oh, Jonathan, this is super! Let's go over that next hill – there – come on. It's not far – oh, this is like heaven!'

'It's like dreaming,' whispered Jonathan, floating, his eyes shut. 'Let's hold hands.'

Hand in hand they floated gently together over the brow of the next hill, their feet just brushing the tops of the tallest grasses, their shadows trailing long and slanting behind them. Larks rose twittering and shrilling their surprise from underneath and a flock of crows high above cawed and croaked their amazement, to see the humans drift so easily with the wind.

'Keep away, keep away, there's enchantment about, watch out,' they warned each other, and scattered to different quarters of the sky.

3

'Wonder what's disturbed those crows?' said Dave as he and Ron toiled up the hill.

'Don't know, Dave. Could be a dog up there or something. It's hardly likely to be anything of interest, I suppose.'

'No. Birds don't take much notice of Them.'

'Unless the object is *very* near,' put in Ron, a little wistfully. He knew that Dave was the real expert, having actually had a sighting, near this very spot last summer. It had been a summer evening and Dave had seen the UFO distinctly as it streaked low across the sky, heading west. He hadn't been able to take a picture, as he hadn't had his camera with him as was so often the maddening case with the best sightings. Nevertheless this undoubted sighting had given Dave a distinct authority over Ron and indeed in their local branch of the Flying Saucer and Extra Terrestrial Society. And then only last week Mr Donaldson, the president, while he was doing his morning exercises near the bedroom window had seen a silver streak zig-zag soundlessly across the sky, and then travel at incredible velocity towards the rising sun.

Dawn, and very early morning were good times for Them to make contact. So Dave and Ron were out fully equipped this time with a camera, a compass, a tape recorder, and a pair of binoculars, everything necessary for a truly scientific observation. Ron's landlady, who was the motherly kind, had cut them sandwiches and made a flask of coffee, and they could observe for hours if necessary.

Of course the best thing of all would be if a machine landed, and Ron and Dave could, as representatives of the human race, parley with its crew. Such a thing had been known to happen; sometimes even, earth men and women were invited into the spacecraft – though again it was unfortunate that nobody had succeeded in taking a photograph of this.

Thoughts such as these were running through Ron's head as he paused to put the binoculars to his eyes and slowly sweep the surrounding heavens. Something black; he focused on a crow, he could see its wing feathers distinctly. He lowered the binoculars to the crest of the hill – what was this? Another crow – but it was *huge*. The sun, still not far from the horizon of the hill, lit up the flying shape from behind, gilding it and dazzling Ron's eyes. Then the shape was gone, dipping back behind the hill.

'Dave! The camera!' Ron shouted incoherently. 'I've seen something!'

He lowered the binoculars, but there was nothing to be seen with the naked eye, only the grass at the top of the hill and the crows, high up now, wheeling in different directions.

'What?' Dave came panting up to Ron, who was a few paces in advance. 'Where?'

'It's gone now. But it was definitely an object out of this world, Dave. It was two headed, a kind of rearing black shape.'

Dave held his camera at the ready. 'It didn't look to you like any kind of alien craft?'

'Definitely not, Dave. It would be one of the aliens themselves, perhaps flying separately on machinery attached to the legs. There were four legs – I think,' added Ron, trying to visualize the very fleeting image his eyes had received.

'We'd better get to the top of the hill fast,' said Dave resolutely, and began to run and scramble as quickly as he could. The hill was very steep at this point with winding sheep tracks over the turf, and bare patches of chalky-white earth. When they reached the top they were both sweating and out of breath.

'There's a good view from here,' panted Ron, the binoculars to his eyes. 'You can see back over the valley – all smoothed out from where the glaciers came – and up to the next crest. What's that? Oh, just a sheep moving. I'm focusing it on those hawthorn bushes now – oh, another sheep. Perhaps the alien's craft could be far beyond – somewhere in that clump of beeches.'

They stood in silence for a few minutes until Dave became a little restive. 'I'm going to have a sit down and some coffee,' he said, suiting the action to the words. 'Of course, Ron, you must bear in mind the possibility that it was a hang glider you saw. They do hang glide from these Downs.'

'No – it wasn't a hang glider – definitely not,' said Ron, rather hurt. 'I know what *they* look like, and this wasn't in the least like.'

'Have some coffee,' said Dave. 'What's in those sandwiches, then?'

But Ron disdained food and stood above Dave, continuing to rake the countryside with his binoculars.

'Let's go back to Mr and Mrs Tom, we're getting a little far away,' Martha said.

And so they floated back, alighting once and jumping again, taking advantage of an upsurge of air and drifting down finally to where Mr Tom was sitting, smoking a diminutive clay pipe, and Mrs Tom was tussling with a tough sprig of wild mint, her back to them.

'Just pick me off a bit of this mint,' she said to them. 'And I want some thyme, too. It's blooming annoying being so small – Put the leaves into the weather house now.'

'Have a good fly?' asked Mr Tom cheerfully. 'Upon my word I envy you. I haven't flown for such a long time.'

'Can't you fly? How is it you can help us to fly and not fly yourself?' asked Martha with concern.

'Ah, that's the question. We can only do as we're asked now, not what *we* want – due to the little misunderstanding I think we've already referred to.'

'Oh, call a spade, a spade,' snapped Mrs Tom. 'It was a punishment if there ever were such a thing.'

'As you say, my dear,' said Mr Tom, the jolly smile leaving his face.

He looked so miserable that Martha burst out, 'If you got

onto our shoulders – or into your house if you like – you could come with us. We could carry the house. Do you think that would work?'

'Certainly,' he said, brightening.

'Come on, then.'

'Don't tilt the house, mind,' warned Mrs Tom. She and Mr Tom climbed inside it and stood by the doors, holding on tightly.

'We can bind ourselves on with only a very little pinch of power,' said Mr Tom gaily to his wife. 'I really believe we'll be allowed to do that. I don't see how the Powers that be could object.'

'Hrm,' she sniffed, as if in disbelief, but appeared quite ready to be borne aloft.

'Come on, then, Martha, Jonathan, what are you waiting for? You can each take one side with one hand only – it'll work, you'll see.'

The house had become so light that Martha and Jonathan found this a perfectly possible way of going and so they rose in the air, higher than they had ever been and then drifted away, slowly descending. They crossed the valley into which Ron had been looking only minutes before and approached the brow of the hill beyond, where cloud and sun were rapidly alternating. A cool wind was blowing now, ruffling the long grasses this way and that, and they blew with it, rapidly approaching a slight depression in the ground, just off the crest of the hill where Dave and Ron had gone to eat their breakfast.

Ron, still a little hurt by Dave's putting his stomach before the need for constant observation, had decided that he had better take a little nourishment himself, before Dave finished it all up. After all, whose landlady had made the sandwiches anyway?

'Mind out!'

Jonathan's legs kicked up and he threw himself sideways to avoid the top of Dave's head as he drifted directly over him. Dave and Ron were sitting with their backs against the wind, and almost totally hidden by the depression in the ground.

'Hey – what are you doing?' Jonathan lurched partly on top of the house, pushing Martha down to make an awkward landing in a low hawthorn bush. Somehow they managed to keep the house more or less upright.

'Good day to you!' Mr Tom genially took off his hat and waved it politely at Dave and Ron who, half-eaten sandwiches in their hands, had risen to their knees in astonishment.

'Don't greet them, you fool,' cried Mrs Tom, brandishing her umbrella at her husband. 'They're not supposed to see us, remember. We're only for *children*. Get off again, Martha. Jonathan, do. Jump, idiots, jump!'

Martha and Jonathan, collecting their wits, jumped, and a particularly strong gust of wind arising then, were whisked off sideways, only a few feet from the ground.

'The camera, Dave, the camera!' shrieked Ron, throwing away his sandwich in a mad hunt for his binoculars. Where had he put them?

'Here, I have it here.' Dave, his hands shaking, held out his camera, busily adjusted it, put it to his eye. He couldn't hold it very still, but 'click' *here* was surely a picture, and 'click' another, and 'click' another – no, the aliens had disappeared into a wood. He had lost them. Never mind, he did have the pictures. What were the aliens? They had come and gone so swiftly – he – he didn't know what they were or what to think. He hadn't had time to see them properly and the sun had been in his eyes.

Ron cast down his binoculars. He had not succeeded in focusing them correctly in time anyway. But he knew what he had seen.

'What an extraordinary thing,' he said reflectively, almost dreamily, to Dave.

'Flying aliens, larger than their spacecraft, *carrying* their spacecraft, in fact. This opens up totally new dimensions, Dave. Nobody's ever seen anything like that before.'

'I don't get it, Ron. I must admit – do you think they practised some kind of hypnotism? For it seemed to me – not only were the aliens carrying their spacecraft – but – correct me if I'm wrong – *inside* the spacecraft were yet more aliens, much smaller – who cried out instructions to the large ones.'

'Yes, I noted that, Dave. You've got to remember – size is only relative – meaningless, in a way – but do you think the small ones were actually the masters of the larger ones? Two different races on the same planet, perhaps?'

'Or two different planets. Do you think we shall ever know?'

'The eye can be a great deceiver,' said Ron solemnly. 'It may be they cast some sort of a cloak of illusion over our eyes. But we have your record of the incident, Dave. The camera cannot lie.'

'No, the camera cannot lie. I took at least two pictures,' exclaimed Dave, patting his camera with a sense of great achievement. Then a horrible thought struck him. He bent down to investigate.

'Oh no!'

'What is it?'

'I've got two pictures all right. But they'll be two pictures of the inside of the lens cap. I forgot to take the bloody thing off!'

'Oh, Dave! But we – we know what we saw, don't we?'

'Nobody will ever believe us,' said Dave with a sudden melancholy insight. 'UFOs streaking across the sky – that's one thing. But that – what we saw – that's a bit much, even for the Society. Do you think that any of them are going to believe us? We haven't any evidence at all – '

'If only it had been a normal UFO, hovering in the sky for a time, and we'd been in less of a rush!' exclaimed Ron wistfully.

'My only thought, Ron, is to examine the ground under where the aliens landed. They could have had some kind of anti-gravity machinery attached to their legs; something that burnt the grass beneath them as they zoomed off. That might give us a little proof.'

'It was somewhere round this bush,' cried Ron hopefully, going over to it, then shaking his head in disappointment. 'Nothing: the grass isn't even flattened.'

'What's this?' exclaimed Dave, pouncing on it.

But when they examined the white object Dave had found

they both had to admit it couldn't have had anything to do with the aliens at all.

No alien would drop a clean white handkerchief, neatly marked in one corner with the name "Martha Grant".

'You've gone and lost me the sheet off my bed,' grumbled Mrs Tom, 'tilting the house like that. People should be more careful when they fly. *Not* a very well managed wish at all. That's your fault, Tom.'

'I didn't know I was supposed to be managing it,' replied Mr Tom mildly.

'Another time we must arrange it better between ourselves. All I know is, I'm not doing the next one. It's set fine for several days now and even when I'm awake the weather does affect me. I need a good long sleep – when Martha gets me that clean sheet.'

'Will this do?' Martha produced another clean handkerchief from her drawer. It had a rather pretty decoration of rosebuds in one corner.

'Passable,' sniffed Mrs Tom, examining it. 'Mind you, it's nothing like what I'm used to. Oh, for my beautiful linen sheets, all smelling of lavender – when will I feel you again? Oh, well it's no good crying over spilt milk. And now before that sun gets any more glaring, I'll retire. First wish over and completed. Please don't have another for a day or so, there's a good girl.'

And with a brief nod to Martha, she retired to the back of the weather house.

'The wish is all over then?' said Martha a little wistfully to Mr Tom. 'We won't be able to fly again?'

Mr Tom looked vague and scratched his head. 'You could use up another wish on it if you really wanted,' he said. 'But we can't make flying a permanent condition for you, no. It's hard to keep up a wish for longer than a few hours, even with both of us concentrating.'

'Oh.'

Martha considered the matter. That certainly explained why she and Jonathan had been able to fly less and less on the way home. They had ended by jumping and floating a few paces and then by walking. She had thought their failing powers were perhaps due to the necessity for keeping their skills concealed from other people: certainly once they were on the road which led to their village there had been an increasing amount of cars and lorries about, and a few people on bicycles.

By the time they had reached home it was nearly eight o'clock. Curtains were being undrawn in both Martha's house and Jonathan's when they sneaked in. But by good fortune Martha had been able to return to her room without anybody knowing she had been out of it. Whether Jonathan had been as lucky, she had no idea. But Jonathan had a general talent for keeping out of trouble; perhaps because he was quiet and unobtrusive and looked more honest and good than he in fact was. Martha had often envied him this quality at school.

'Goodness, I'm hungry!' she said to Mr Tom, who was standing smoking his pipe at the door of his house. 'I feel as if I've already had most of today! Do you want me to bring you and Mrs Tom any breakfast?'

'Regretfully not,' he shook his head. 'We need no food now, and hardly any drink. My wife is an excellent cook; ah me! I suppose we are justly punished. At least I can enjoy my pipe still.'

'Will you be all right if I leave you and go downstairs to breakfast?' Martha asked him.

'Perfectly, my dear, thank you. We change into wood in the twinkling of an eye if anybody strange comes in. We need now nothing but a little time to rest and gather our strength. We will let you know when we are ready for another wish.'

'That's all right,' said Martha. 'I don't know that I would want another one right away. All I want right now is my breakfast. I'm going to go downstairs and put the kettle on and hurry things up a bit. Everybody is so slow and lazy in this house during holidays.'

And in all the priggish virtue of the early riser who has accomplished a great deal while everybody else lies hoggishly abed, Martha ran downstairs.

4

'Now, Martha, what are your plans today?' said her mother briskly at the breakfast table two days later.

'I don't know yet,' said Martha, giving a great yawn. 'It's not a very nice day, is it?'

Outside the kitchen window rain was pelting down from a grey overcast sky.

'I know,' said Mrs Grant. 'It would rain today, wouldn't it? It's the fête this afternoon. It rained last year too on the fête day; I do think it's bad luck to get another wet day.'

'It's going to clear up this afternoon, according to the radio,' said the one of Martha's brothers who was downstairs and having breakfast.

'Mark! Not so much sugar on your cereal, *please*!' interjected his mother. She switched her attention back to Martha.

'I just wanted to know what you were thinking of doing; because as you know I'll be all tied up with the White Elephant stall at the fête: I'm helping Mollie Anderson. Were you thinking of coming to the fête?'

'If you give me some money to spend,' said Martha. 'I never have *any* money.' Then she was struck with a brilliant idea. 'Why – ' she said, but stopped just in time.

'You can have 50p,' said her father, rising and pushing his chair aside. 'And another 25p if you promise to go to the bottle stall for me: last year you and Mark won that bottle of whisky. That was a good fête that was.'

'Are you showing any of your pictures, Daddy?' asked Martha. 'Can I help you choose one?'

'Oh *no*,' groaned Mark. 'Daddy's pictures are embarrassing – at least ...' He caught sight of his father's hurt

29

expression. 'I mean it's embarrassing having a father who paints pictures and will show them round the place – especially when they never win a prize.'

'One has to have the also-rans in any competition,' said Mr Grant, a little sadly.

'I think you're beastly, Mark. Daddy's pictures are lovely,' cried Martha, hot in her father's defence.

Mr Grant painted very small watercolours in pale colours. Each picture seemed to come out smaller than the one before. He painted flowers and little domestic scenes; the dog on a chair, a bowl of fruit, part of the outside of their house, a view from a window, that kind of thing. Martha was his greatest fan; already she had three of his paintings in her room.

'Once I sold a picture for £5,' said Mr Grant reflectively.

'Will the pictures at the fête be on sale?' asked Martha, hugging her idea to her.

'Oh yes, I'm entering two, as a matter of fact. I'm going to take them along this morning. You can come and help me make the final selection if you like.'

'Good,' said Mrs Grant, beaming amiably on husband and daughter alike. 'That's got you two settled then . . . Mark, are you going?'

'Helping Anna and her silly friend with the pony rides,' mumbled Mark through a large mouthful of toast. 'They're paying me – or I don't do it.'

'You should help at our village fête without any thought of reward –' his mother was beginning severely when Anna burst into the room, in her dressing gown and slippers.

Anna was in one of her early morning smouldering rages.

'Mummy, you are to tell Paul not to play that filthy record player so loudly,' she gritted through clenched teeth. 'It goes through and through my head. I was just having the small pleasure of a nice dream, I don't often get *them*, when I was blasted out by this awful din. He just lies in bed with it full on and doesn't take any notice of anybody else. It's so selfish.'

'At least it got you up,' retorted her mother unsympathetically. 'And what a way to come down to breakfast, Anna! You haven't even put a comb through your hair.'

'*And* it's raining,' grumbled Anna, staring out of the window. 'We'll all get soaked; pneumonia as like as not. Imagine dragging two ponies through the mud with hordes of drenched kids on their backs! Oh, it's not fair!'

'You'll have to pay me more if it's raining hard,' said Mark swiftly. 'Or I don't help.'

'Oh, you beastly boy!' cried his mother.

Martha left the breakfast table with her father, feeling unpleasantly superior. She would call on Jonathan right away and tell him her plan. It would be the best wish ever; in fact she could not think why they hadn't started with it.

'All right, so it's not a chest of treasure, or a million pounds,' said Jonathan when she put the idea to him half an hour later. 'It's something we can spend easily, right away, without questions being asked. I get the point.'

'I think the easiest thing would be 50p pieces,' cried Martha excitedly. 'It was Daddy saying he's give me 50p for the fête that made me think of it. Nobody thinks anything of one having a few 50p pieces. We can word it so the wish gives us them just as we want them.'

'Yes – that's not a bad idea,' said Jonathan a little grudgingly. 'Come on, let's get on with it. There are lots of things I want to buy.'

So Martha and Jonathan went upstairs to Martha's room to find Mrs Tom busily surveying Martha's collection of books. She had managed to clamber from one shelf to another and was poised on the second shelf, her head sideways so she could read the titles of the books on their spines.

'Ah,' she said briskly on seeing Martha. 'Just bring this collection of fairy tales out for me, there's a good girl. I want to see how they're telling them these days.'

'We want to make our second wish now, please,' said Martha as she spread the book out on the floor for Mrs Tom.

'What's that? In good time. I'm busy, as you can see. Very crude colouring, isn't it? Sleeping Beauty – what a silly drawing. She didn't look in the least like that you know . . .'

'We want to wish for money,' said Jonathan, now as excited and impatient as Martha.

'Of course the modern idea of beauty is totally wrong,' said Mrs Tom, standing critically on the coloured picture, somewhere in the region of Sleeping Beauty's stomach. 'All that silly golden hair. What's the matter with a good strong black?' and she smoothed her own black locks complacently.

'Money in 50p pieces – I can show you one if you don't know what they look like,' cried Martha.

'What's that? A money wish? How very worldly and boring of you.'

'You mean you won't do it?' Martha's face fell, and she sank to the floor imploringly beside Mrs Tom. 'Oh, please, please do it! Would it be easier if we asked for gold then, or jewellery?'

'Of course I can do it,' sniffed Mrs Tom instantly, as if she had been insulted. 'I can do it any way you say. But don't expect it to be a roaring success. These money wishes never work out like that.'

'But we've discussed that. It's because people wish everything they touch to be turned to gold, or have old-fashioned coins which have to be changed,' cried Jonathan. 'We aren't so stupid as that. Martha even thinks it might be silly to have notes which people might think were forgeries, or wonder how we got so many.'

'But just a few 50p pieces,' interjected Martha, 'just as we wanted them – how could that go wrong?'

'How indeed?' said Mrs Tom drily, giving them her full attention at last. 'Especially as it's me doing it and not that fool of a husband of mine. You can disregard *him* for the day – he's got rheumatism with the damp and he's sleeping it off in our house. I approve of you giving careful thought to the wording of the wish, at least. Words are extremely important things. So come along then, say them.'

Martha took a deep breath, 'We wish for 50p pieces, just enough to cover whatever we want to buy, and we wish for them to appear just *before* we buy whatever it is – because we don't want to go about with great heavy hoards of them in our pockets.'

'Show her the 50p piece,' whispered Jonathan. So Martha

held up the coin and Mrs Tom nodded and wrote something in her notebook.

'Wish number two granted,' she said.

'Oh.' Martha looked about her vaguely: nothing had happened.

'Don't be silly – nothing will happen until we've got something we want to buy,' Jonathan reminded her. 'Let's go and make a list now – a list of all the things we want.'

'Don't forget – you'll have to take us with you when you go shopping,' Mrs Tom reminded them. 'It's part of the contract. We can't be far away while the wish works itself out.'

'Yes, yes,' cried Martha and Jonathan as they hunted for paper and a pencil. This was going to be the shopping list to end all shopping lists . . .

At two o'clock the sun came out, pushing its way aggressively between the clouds as if it meant to stay. The front door of the Grants' house opened and shut as in ones and twos they all left to go to the fête. Martha, followed by Toby the dog, was last.

'Toby, you can't come with me, you're too much nuisance,' she said to him at the gate, but Toby took no notice. He was a black-and-white fox-terrier type mongrel who was nearly as old as Martha and had not the least intention of being bossed about by her. Martha was carrying the weatherhouse in a large carrier bag, and Mr and Mrs Tom were for the time being wooden figures only: Mrs Tom outside the house, her umbrella up, Mr Tom within. If it kept fine they might change position.

As she passed Jonathan's house and neat front garden Jonathan ran out to meet her, and they began the quarter of a mile walk to the village green together. They were going to the fête because it was their only chance of buying anything more.

When Martha had made the wish, as she thought so carefully and cleverly, she had forgotten one thing. It was Saturday, and it was the day of the fête. Neither of her parents was going into town that morning in the car – and the only bus had already left. It was a long way to bicycle: some of the roads were dangerous and neither Martha nor Jonathan were as yet allowed on them.

So they were stuck in the village – with unlimited money – but nowhere much to spend it. The village shop was their only hope – and it shut at lunch time.

So Martha and Jonathan had visited the village shop. It did sell a few things besides food. They each had bought a huge box of chocolates: they had bought sweets, they had bought crayons and notepaper, they had bought ice creams, they had bought batteries for Jonathan's torch – they had bought – There hadn't been much else it sold that they had wanted. Who would want to buy detergent or matches or shoe laces? Margarine or flour or bacon?

'Oh, why don't we live in a really big city!' exclaimed Martha passionately when they came out of the shop with all their things. 'Just think what we could be getting. How can I buy a pony in the *village shop*.' The scorn in her voice when she came to 'village shop' was intense.

'It doesn't even sell skateboards,' agreed Jonathan mournfully. 'Oh – *blast!*' He had dropped one of his purchases. Even though their buying spree had had its limitations, they nevertheless had more than they could comfortably carry.

After the village shop, Jonathan had the idea of visiting a friend of his who was selling his model train set: Martha was obliged to trail with him to the far end of the village – where he found his friend and all his family out for the day. So, tired, and not quite so elated with their shopping spree as they had thought to be, they had returned home for lunch.

And here they were, fed and rested, sallying forth to spend, spend as madly as one can at a village fête which has things like coconut shies, hot dogs, pony rides, lucky draws, produce stalls, home-made food, handicraft and art shows – but not much else.

It was frustrating not to be in a big city but when they reached the village green and heard the band (local, amateur, and named The Rustic Roarers) blaring out over the loudspeakers, both of them felt in much better spirits.

'Just think if it was a proper fair though,' said Jonathan

wistfully. 'Instead of trying to knock down silly coconuts which one never can, or guess the weight of some cake, we could be on the Dodgems or the Big Dipper. Oh, why do we have to live in a boring old village?'

'But I do like villages and countryside sometimes,' said Martha thoughtfully, and then: 'Let's have some candy floss, shall we? And they've got a second bookstall again this year. I'm going to get some books from that.'

An hour or so passed very pleasantly. Both Martha and Jonathan had candy floss and ice cream and acquired a pile of books, and Martha bought a plant in a pot. Then they had several goes at the bottle stall – you had to pay 25p for a selection of playing cards and if you were very lucky you got the very same card a bottle was standing on, and claimed the bottle for your own. Of course the bottles were of any kind at all, and so you could win tomato ketchup or hair spray or nail varnish as well as lemonade, or if you were very lucky, wine or whisky.

After Martha had spent about three pounds, she found she had won a large bottle of beer, a bottle of brown sauce and a bottle of carpet shampoo – not a particularly attractive haul and one which was awkward to carry, considering that she also had six books of various sizes and the carrier bag with the weather house, and the plant in its pot.

She staggered past her mother at the White Elephant stall without recognizing her.

'Hey! Martha!' her mother called. 'Good lord, you *are* weighed down. What have you won? Ugh – what a nasty sauce. The other things will be useful. Don't let your father get at the beer; I'd like some for myself later on. Martha! Don't go. I want your help for a while. Mollie's had to go off for ten minutes and I want somebody to help with the change. Put all your things down there . . . Can I help you?' She had moved to a corner of the stall. 'This lovely vase of artificial flowers? Only 35p, Martha, the change is in the bowl, over there. Thank you.'

Martha quite enjoyed helping at the White Elephant stall.

There was such a crowd that she had lost sight of Jonathan, who had wandered off with some other boys from the local school to try their hand at the coconut shy and the hoop-la stalls. Soon Mollie Anderson returned and they agreed that Martha's mother could have a ten minute break in her turn. Then Jonathan turned up, equally laden down with books, bottles and a coconut which he said proudly that he had won after forty-two goes, and took his turn at being a stall keeper while Martha wandered off into the marquee which held all the garden produce and flower arrangements and works of art which had been entered for prizes. There were home-made cakes and bread and bottles of home-made wine and corn dollies and knitted garments and at the far end, a picture show, near which she saw her father loitering and talking to a fellow artist. He had not won a prize, though Martha felt he ought to have done. Why, his painting of the apple tree with Toby lying below it was far better than any of the others. The judges simply didn't know their business. Not one of the paintings displayed the red spot on one corner which meant they had been sold.

Martha had a brilliant idea; one of her best. Drunk now with spending, she had no inhibitions. *She* would buy her father's pictures; she wouldn't tell him or any of her family. She could give it away to somebody. Her father would think a rich patron had appeared, and would be overcome with delight. It would be Martha and Jonathan's secret.

She waited until her father, with a last rather selfconscious look around, had left the tent. Then she went up to the woman in charge.

'I'd like to buy that picture,' she said grandly.

'What's that, dear?' said the woman with a sugary smile. She was not someone Martha knew; a rather fat middle-aged blonde wearing a tight pink dress. 'I don't think any of them are for sale.'

'They were last year,' said Martha shortly. The fool of a woman obviously didn't know her own business.

'Well maybe they were – but I'm sure they'll all be too expensive for you, dear. The frames alone are quite a price, you know.'

36

'I want to buy that picture,' said Martha firmly. 'It'll be about five pounds and I've got the money.'

'Just a moment,' said the woman with another rather dubious look at Martha. She went and had a whispered conversation with a man sitting at a trestle table in the background.

'Yes, it is five pounds,' she said, coming back. 'It seems an awful lot for a little girl like you to spend.'

'I'm *not* a little girl!' flashed Martha, deeply hurt and insulted. How maddeningly patronizing this woman was! Why should grown-ups think they had the right to treat children like that?

'Here is the money,' she said with great dignity, drawing her purse from her pocket. It felt almost empty but filled as she opened it and she handed over the coins grandly, without counting them.

'There's only four pounds fifty here, dear,' said the blonde, after a minute of reckoning. 'Only nine fifties. You need to give me ten for five pounds, don't you?'

'I *know* ten fifties make five pounds!' cried Martha in confusion. She searched in her purse, feeling a hot blood of mingled annoyance and self-consciousness flood her cheeks. Her desperate fingers met one more coin and she handed it over.

'Oh, but this isn't any good, dear,' said the woman in even more patronizing tones. 'This is an old half crown. It's not legal tender now, is it?'

'I know it isn't,' said Martha, beet red, snatching it back. She searched her purse desperately, but nothing else appeared apart from one very old-looking penny with Queen Victoria's head on it. What was Mrs Tom about? Where *was* Mrs Tom?

At that moment it flashed on Martha that the bag containing the weather house was some way away at the White Elephant stall. She had put it down with all her other things and forgotten all about it.

In the meanwhile there were no other coins of any other kind forthcoming from her purse. She searched her pockets, nothing there.

She did not know what she would have done had she not seen Jonathan wandering about further down the tent among the home-made wines, where his mother had won a prize.

She ran to him urgently. 'Jonathan, have you any money? I must have 50p!'

'All right.' He produced it from his pocket, turning over the rest of his change. He had some 1p and 2p pieces, but nothing else. 'That's funny. I thought I'd more than that. But I expect several more will come along if I want to buy anything.'

'I wouldn't be too sure of that,' said Martha as she ran back with the coin.

'All right, dear,' said the blonde. 'The picture is yours now. It's quite a pleasant little scene, isn't it? Are you going to hang it in your room? It will have to stay here for the rest of the show of course, and you can come and fetch it afterwards.'

'Yes, yes,' cried Martha, whose one thought now was to return to the White Elephant stall.

'That Mrs Anderson and your Mum said they didn't need me any more,' said Jonathan as they pushed their way out of the marquee. 'That's why I came along.'

They ran to the White Elephant stall which was beginning to look a lot emptier. Most of the sprays of artificial flowers had gone, and the tea cosies and some china. There were a few things left like dusty old clocks which didn't work, and hideous ornaments and raffia bags. On the grass behind the stall Martha saw her pile of belongings, the books, the plant pot, Jonathan's things too. But where, oh where was the plastic carrier bag which had contained the weather house?

Where was the weather house?

'What are you looking for, Martha?' asked Mrs Anderson rather sharply.

'There was a weather house, with a little man and wife – you know,' exclaimed Martha in anguish, one dreadful thought running through her head.

'Oh – You mean the one on the stall? It was in a bag on the end of the stall and I thought it was a donation to the stall. Do you mean to tell me you didn't want it to be sold?'

'No, of course not – You don't mean you have – ' cried Martha frantically.

'Why, yes of course. I sold that about ten minutes ago. It was on the stall – how did it come to be on the stall if you didn't want it sold?'

'I don't know,' cried poor Martha almost in tears.

'Who did you sell it to?' put in Jonathan, suppressing an urge to take Mrs Anderson by the arm and shake her.

'Oh, I don't know. I'm afraid I didn't notice particularly,' she said vaguely. 'Let me think – was it a woman and her little girl? Yes, that's right, a woman with a little girl of about four or five.'

'What did the woman look like?' cried Martha and Jonathan together.

'Well – I suppose she was about my age . . . dark, going grey. A flowered jacket I think – I don't really know any more than that.'

'We *must* find her – them,' Martha and Jonathan said to one another as they left the stall and stared desperately round the fête ground.

'Stupid woman!' muttered Jonathan vindictively of Mrs Anderson. 'Same age as *I* am! How old *is* the old bag anyway?'

'Dark, and a flowered jacket and with a little girl,' Martha reminded him. 'It shouldn't be as difficult as all that. If only there weren't so many people here. It's confusing. And I'm tired and I wish I hadn't had that candy floss and stuff.'

'I'm thirsty and I've got indigestion,' Jonathan said, pushing his hair back from his dirty, sweating forehead. 'And, Martha, I've just thought. What if that little girl of four or five starts making wishes? Will the Toms have to grant them? Will they go over to her? Have we lost them for ever?'

'She might wish *anything*,' cried Martha in horror, surveying the crowds of men, women and children wandering in all directions.

'A child that age has no sense at all. Suppose she wished for something entirely mad – like – like for someone to drop dead, or for the sun to fall out of the sky – would the Toms be bound to grant it?' persisted Jonathan.

'Oh, do shut up! We'll just have to find them – if they've not got into some car and driven off heaven knows where!'

But this possibility was too awful for them to contemplate.

'They *must* be still at the fête,' said Jonathan grimly. 'And we're going to find them if it kills us.'

A dreadful hour dragged by. They looked everywhere. They visited the pony ride with its long queue of children, where Anna, her girl friend and Mark, all three hot and red-faced, were grimly leading the two ponies to and fro with the children proudly clinging to their manes. Here they found Toby the dog who, tail waving jauntily, was weaving in and out under the ponies' hooves, presumably thinking he was helping too.

'For God's sake take that awful dog away,' gritted Anna between her teeth. 'What fool let him out anyway?'

'Toby! Toby!' called Martha ineffectually. He merely grinned at her and turned his back. Meanwhile Jonathan found out from Mark that he thought, but was not sure, that the woman with the flowered jacket had given the little girl a ride about five minutes previously.

'Were they carrying anything?' asked Jonathan eagerly, but Mark hadn't noticed particularly. 'Perhaps the woman had a big basket or a carrier bag,' he said vaguely. 'I don't know.'

'Which way did they go?'

'Search me.'

'At least this means they're still around,' said Martha hopefully.

'And the crowd's getting thinner; we *must* see them soon.'

'Oh my legs *ache* so, and my arms, and my head.'

'I wish that beastly hot sun would go in,' said Jonathan crossly, squinting sideways up at it.

'Jonathan – don't *wish*. Suppose the Toms had been within earshot?'

'Suppose the stupid girl is wishing to go home, right this very minute,' he said, sitting down heavily on the grass. 'I'm not going to walk another step.'

Sitting together on the grass they then began to see lots of people they knew, including Jonathan's mother who came up to him and reminded him that time was getting on and she was going home, and that he was not to be late for supper.

'Supper!' said Jonathan bitterly, when she had gone. 'I feel sick. I don't mind if I never eat again!'

'There's Paul,' said Martha listlessly. Paul, the older of her two brothers, was wandering about on his own, looking bored. Seeing them, he came and sat down with them. Some of the stalls were beginning to pack up, their competitions over or their goods sold.

'Are you going to stay for the Grand Draw?' Paul asked. 'Daddy gave me some money for tickets for it, so I'm staying to see if we win anything. They'll be announcing it soon.'

'This woman might be waiting for that too,' said Martha, a little hope coming back to her. 'Come on, Jonathan, let's get nearer to the announcer. That's where people go when they're waiting for the results.'

And, at last, as the announcer's voice began to boom out with a seemingly endless list of prizewinners, they suddenly saw a middle-aged woman in a pink and blue flowered jacket and a blue skirt and white sandals, holding a little girl by the hand. In the other hand she had a large bag which bulged full.

'There they are!' In her relief Martha ran over to them without in the least thinking what she was going to say. However, she managed to stammer out, 'Please, I think you've bought something of mine by mistake. It was on the White Elephant stall, but it should never have been sold.'

'Oh,' said the woman. She had a tight, small mouth and the kind of impassive face which does not change. 'You mean this house. I'd like it for my front room. I paid 75p for it.'

'It's worth far more than that!' cried Martha momentarily side-tracked.

'I don't know about that. That was the price the lady asked.'

'Can we buy it back from you?' Jonathan put in.

'You fool,' Martha whispered to him. 'What with? We've practically no money left.'

'Besides I don't know that I want to sell,' said the woman, her face a shut trap. She turned away from them. The little

41

girl at her side who had been staring unblinkingly at Martha and Jonathan, began to grizzle. 'Nana, I'm tired. I want to go home now.'

'Just wait a minute while Nana hears the results of the Draw,' the woman shushed her.

'I want an ice cream. I wish – '

'No, you don't!'

'Oh, shut up!' Both Martha and Jonathan cried this out together in desperation; Martha's hand flashing out to cover the child's mouth.

Several people turned to look and the woman in the flowered jacket turned on them with a face of thunder. 'Do you mind – ' she began.

'I *wish* you'd give me the weather house,' Martha suddenly said, realizing her only way out of the increasingly difficult situation.

The woman's face was then a sight worth seeing. The wish was obviously quite against her natural inclination and character. Looking anxious, as if she were about to burst into tears, she rummaged in her bag and brought out the weather house. Mrs Tom had withdrawn a little way, and Mr Tom could be seen near the entrance. Both of them stared woodenly and lifelessly up at the sky.

'If you want it so much you can have it,' she cried. 'No, I don't want the money back. I'm glad to be rid of it; it'll bring me bad luck if I keep it. You take it. Come on, Sharon.'

So saying, she pulled the astonished Sharon round, thrust the weather house into Martha's eager hands and walked off, shaking her head and muttering to herself.

'Why did you give it away?' Martha heard Sharon say as they disappeared into the crowd.

'I don't know. I've never done anything like that before. It just came to me that those things can be unlucky. Come on, *do*, Sharon. No we're *not* waiting for any more results. I've not won anything. It's not my day today. I want to get back home and put my feet up.'

She had gone.

'Well,' said Martha and Jonathan weakly to one another.

They collected all their possessions, including the picture, and began to walk home, followed at a little distance by Toby, who had something in his mouth.

'That your terrier?' said a man to Martha. 'He's just had my kiddie's hot dog off him. Took it right out of his hand . . .'

'Not my dog, no,' said Martha, walking as quickly as she could and not looking behind. She was nearly dead with fatigue and with the weight of all the things she was carrying.

'We bought too much,' were Jonathan's only words as they limped slowly together down the lane.

'At least Toby had a good fête,' said Martha thoughtfully, watching him trot eagerly past them, the hot dog still in his mouth. 'I wonder what it's like to be Toby. I wish – Oh, no, I don't.'

'I don't wish *anything*,' said Jonathan wearily.

And then, as Jonathan was speaking, it suddenly struck Martha. They had, of course, totally mismanaged the entire day.

'Oh my golly!' she cried. 'Why didn't we think of it? Why on earth didn't we? And it's far too late now.'

'Think of what?'

'Don't you see, we didn't get to good shops and shopping, just because we were too stupid to think of the proper way to do it! We could have *wished* ourselves in a town as easily as anything! We could have gone to London *and* back in – in a car or anything, if we'd only thought to say it! But we simply never thought of it.'

'No, we didn't,' said Jonathan blankly. 'I suppose – I don't know – I suppose we thought we'd only got one wish for the day or something.'

'But we *hadn't*,' cried Martha. 'We made a second one, to get the weather house back. If we hadn't gone to the fête we wouldn't have had to make that wish. We could have used it for far better things.'

'*Now* you say it,' said Jonathan bitterly.

'We were just thinking in a straight line, like, like hens with their beaks to the ground; we hadn't really seen all round it,' cried Martha.

'Oh, Martha, if you have any more horrible ideas like that, far too late, I don't want to know about them,' said Jonathan crossly. 'And now I'm going home. Goodbye.'

'Goodbye,' said Martha sadly, staggering up her front path with all her things, the plant in its pot, the weather house, six books and her father's picture. The picture was the one thing she really liked, and that she wouldn't be able to keep. She must think about giving it away later on; in the meantime she pushed it under her bed.

When she went downstairs for supper she found quite a jolly party. Her parents and Anna were sharing a bottle of cheap wine and the boys had been given the beer.

'It's encouraging to have sold another picture,' Mr Grant was saying happily. 'You see, I do have my admirers. I wonder who's bought it? Somebody who appreciates a subtle use of colour, I feel sure! Well, it was a good fête, wasn't it?'

'Exhausting; I'm worn out!' cried most of the rest of his family.

'I'm glad about the picture, Daddy,' said Martha brightening a little, and smiling inwardly to herself. That, at least, had been a good idea on her part. Perhaps also one or two of the secondhand books she had bought would be readable. She would go to bed early, and try them. A bath would be nice, too.

'Wish number two was perfectly satisfactory, I conclude?' said Mrs Tom with one of her sharp looks, when Martha sank wearily, but cleanly, into bed at last. 'I warned you that those money wishes could be tricky, and considering you were so extremely careless as to lose us for a time, I consider that you came out of it pretty well, thanks to my skill and tact.'

Tact? Martha had not noticed anything particularly tactful about Mrs Tom. She opened her mouth to reply, not altogether politely, because of the way the money had run out so early, and then caught Mr Tom's eye. He was leaning against the outside wall of their house, filling his little pipe.

Mr Tom gave Martha a smile, cocked his head in his wife's direction and then shook it very slightly.

Martha changed her mind swiftly.

'No, I've no complaints,' she found herself saying.

'Good night, Martha. Sleep well.'

And, rather to her own surprise, Martha did as she was told.

5

'Was there ever a mother who had more to contend with than me?' cried Mrs Grant, in the dramatic tone of voice which does not necessarily expect an answer. 'I look forward to the weekend, I can't think why, because it's always on a Saturday morning that everything goes wrong! Who would have thought I'd get floods from the washing machine, I can't think where it leaked from this time, *and* a gerbil behind the fridge all on the same morning! And I've lots and lots of shopping to do and cooking for the weekend. It simply isn't fair. Was there ever a woman so put upon?'

Her children stood about her, sympathizing, but also anxious to get quickly out of the range of trouble.

'I've mopped the water by the door and I'd do more but I'm late already. I'm meeting Steve five minutes ago. I must simply race,' cried Anna, her face radiant in anticipation. She had been a changed girl since she had met Steve a few days ago at a disco; sunny natured and sweet in disposition, but her family hadn't benefited too much by this radiance as she had been out a good deal of the time.

'You oughtn't to let Mark bring that gerbil into the kitchen ever,' was Paul's contribution.

'I like that!' cried Mark, instantly hot in defence of himself and his gerbil. 'I was only changing his water. There's a tap or so in the kitchen with water in them. I expect you hadn't noticed – you never wash up. I just had Snuffy on my shoulder at the time and then Martha let Toby in. I told her not to, but she did, so of course he jumped for Snuffy and poor Snuffy went for the only safe place he knows. And if anybody moves that fridge and crushes poor little Snuffy to death, I'll kill them. It's Martha's fault, Mum, it's not mine at all!'

'I like that!' screamed Martha indignantly. 'I didn't even hear you call to me about Toby. I can't be all over the place just when you want me. I was in the loo, if you want to know. Don't I get any peace even in there?'

'Oh, do stop quarrelling!' cried their mother, her hands over her ears. 'Mark, you must try and lure Snuffy out as quickly as you can. It's simply too nerve-wracking having him there all day with Toby wandering in and out and just waiting his chance to pounce. Besides he might gnaw at the wires at the back of the fridge. We'll all have to get out of the kitchen for a time and you must lay a trail of seeds for him to his cage, or something.'

'I'll put a notice on the kitchen door. "Entry forbidden. Loose Gerbil,"' offered Mark eagerly. He lay on his stomach before the fridge trying to peer under it.

'Snuffy, you silly creature! Come here, Snuffy!' he called. 'Oh, I think I can see him. He's simply petrified of that beastly dog. You'll have to take Toby out, Martha.'

'I don't know why it always has to be me to look after Toby,' Martha began to grumble but her mother swiftly intervened.

'Yes, Martha, do please take him right out of the house for a time. Take him for a walk, take him anywhere.'

'But I don't want to go out right now,' Martha began, but then she saw her mother's face and changed her mind.

'All right. I was going to call on Jonathan sometime,' she said. 'Come on, Toby!'

She seized the reluctant dog by the collar and pulled him away from the back of the fridge where he was standing wagging his tail and pushing his nose as far as he could get, emitting long melodious snuffles as he did so, as if to suck in the hiding gerbil as a vacuum cleaner sucks up dust.

'Bad luck, Toby, no little gerbil for your brekky,' said Paul as they passed him. Toby merely made snorting noises and rolled his eyes as he was dragged out through the front of the house by Martha. She couldn't find his lead, so used a piece of string which she found wrapped round one of the banisters in the hall.

By the time she was walking round the side of Jonathan's house to get to the back quarters where she knew she would find him somewhere, the string had broken, but she carried on, speaking sternly to Toby in the somewhat vain hope that he would obey her.

'Heel, Toby. *Not* over that flowerbed. Heel! For goodness sake, Toby!' Toby had just, in his usual shameless manner, lifted his leg against the stone statue of a little girl holding up her skirt and pointing her foot.

Luckily Jonathan had Hercules's hutch closed and Hercules safely inside. Not that Toby was too interested in Hercules. He had met him before on several occasions, and had decided that it was safer and pleasanter to bark at him from a distance rather than get too near and be expected to *do* something about the disconcertingly fierce and big rabbit, who was a match for any cat or small dog who was foolhardy enough to take him on.

So when Toby saw Martha go up to the cage where Jonathan squatted, talking to his favourite, he was suddenly seized by an intractable tickle in the middle of his spine, and sat down at a good distance from the cage, contorting his neck to bite at it, and pushing himself round in circles with his vigorous front legs.

'Hi,' said Martha to Jonathan, looking round his garden as she always did and thinking how much neater and prettier it was than her own. Both Jonathan's parents were constantly working in and outside their house and garden and both were immaculate. If a rose so much as dropped its petals for five minutes they were picked up and carted off to the compost heap by Jonathan's father, and if you sneezed inside the house Jonathan's mother came up with a duster and polished the piece of furniture you had sneezed near. It was surprising that Jonathan was such a normal boy; just as dirty as anybody else and by no means a Mummy's boy. And in some ways Martha envied him the peace and order of his own house, in which nobody ever seemed to shout or quarrel.

'Look at the brute,' said Jonathan, stuffing a carrot through the bars, an affectionate smile on his face. 'He's in a mad mood today, aren't you, Herk, old lad? Do you know I gave him a rotten carrot by mistake a minute ago and he growled at me? Just like a dog. He was telling me off properly! So I had to say I was sorry and give him another one.'

'What did he say then?' asked Martha.

'Oh, he didn't say anything, he just seized it and turned his back on me to eat it in the corner of his hutch. That meant he thought it was a good one. He doesn't like me to see him eating his very best things. You see, I've rumbled you, Herk. I know all about your most innermost thoughts,' said Jonathan dotingly.

'Gracious, I wouldn't like to *think* what Toby's innermost thoughts are,' exclaimed Martha, trying to stretch out her hand for Toby's collar when she thought he wasn't watching her. Instantly he sprang to his feet, removed himself out of her reach, and cheerfully, grinning happily the while, kicked out with his back legs so that his toenails dug parallel tracks out of the neat lawn.

'What now? What shall we do now?' Toby appeared to be asking, his head slightly on one side. 'I'm ready for anything.'

'Oh, Toby, you are awful. You just don't seem to care at all, and you always seem to have fun. I wonder what it's like being you? I wish I – Jonathan, do you remember, I nearly wished this the other day? It would be most terribly interesting to know what it's like to be an animal, wouldn't it?'

'What – you mean – ' Jonathan's mouth dropped open momentarily while he thought.

'Yes!' He startled both Martha and Toby by suddenly shouting. 'Yes! Let's make that a proper wish. You can be Toby and I'll be Hercules. Just for a time. It'll be fantastic. And we know it won't go on too long because none of the wishes do.'

'But what'll happen to them – I mean the real Toby or Hercules,' said Martha doubtfully. 'It would be awful if it killed them.'

'Why should it do that? I'm sure Mr and Mrs Tom can manage it all right if we say it properly.'

'Yes.' said Martha thoughtfully. This animal wish would be a good joint wish: she had often wondered what it was like being a dog and at times envied Toby. He didn't have to dress and wash and go to school – his life was all games and walks and food. Rather disgusting food sometimes, but then he seemed to like it.

'Yes, all right,' she said again. 'Shall I go and fetch the Toms? They are awake, I heard them arguing in bed while I was dressing for breakfast. Shall I bring them here, or will your mum come out and see them?'

'Bring them here. My mum is in the kitchen all morning baking. And the kitchen looks onto the patio at the side of the house, as you know. She won't see us. Does your mum spend all morning baking?'

'No,' replied Martha. 'She's too busy running in and out saying she's having a dreadful time. Like gerbils behind the fridge.'

'OK, Martha. Hurry and get the Toms then. I'll keep Toby here. Got you!'

And Jonathan surprised Toby by the suddenness of his lunge and had him by the collar while Martha ran home.

Mr and Mrs Tom were still arguing as she carried them into Jonathan's garden.

' – so sloppy, such a waste of time,' she heard Mrs Tom say.

'That's all very well,' he replied in a grumbling tone of voice. 'But what's time for anyway? You tell me that. You simply don't understand, that's your trouble.'

'Understand!' Mrs Tom's voice shrilled up. 'I understand only too well! I understand a lot more about you than you realize, my good fellow!'

'Martha – have you got a transistor radio there? What are those voices?'

Martha froze in horror. She was just outside the kitchen window, on the crazy paving patio where the statue of the little girl stood on its pedestal in a bed of herbs and had completely forgotten Jonathan's mother baking within. Her face was at the window now, looking a little flushed and irritated.

'A radio – yes,' called Martha as cheerfully as she could, remembering with relief that Jonathan's mother was short-sighted and that she was not wearing her glasses.

'Please don't play it too loudly in the garden,' continued Jonathan's mother. 'It's so disturbing for the neighbours – at least – ' She paused and Martha could see the thought come into her face that the nearest neighbours were Martha's own family who were presumably used to the noise made by their own children.

'At least . . .' repeated Jonathan's mother rather vaguely, and then Martha was relieved to see her shrug her shoulders and sigh, as if it was all too much for her, and turn back to her baking.

'Sh!' she hissed reprovingly to Mr and Mrs Tom, who stopped talking and looked suitably chastened as she carried them through the gap in the box hedge which acted as a partial screen between the front garden and the back.

In the back garden she found Jonathan sitting in front of Hercules's partially opened hutch, still holding Toby by the collar, and when he saw Martha approaching, carrying the weather house, he let Toby go.

Martha did not know how it happened, but one moment she was carrying the house with Mr and Mrs Tom looking out of their respective doors, the next, a wildly barking Toby had got between her legs and tripped her, upsetting the weather house. The next minute Toby was running off down the garden bearing Mr Tom in his mouth, much as he had carried the hot dog back from the fête.

'Stop him!' Mrs Tom left the house and ran down the path, brandishing her umbrella, a tiny, impotent figure, and Jonathan and Martha ran too.

'Wish! Wish!' screamed the distraught Mrs Tom up at Martha. 'Don't you see that's the only way to save him? He has no power of his own without your wishes. That beastly dog could kill him like a rat. Oh, wish!'

Martha shuddered. She had seen Toby kill a rat more than once. A quick shake to break the rat's neck and it was over in seconds. Without giving herself time to think about the wording of it, she cried out the wish she and Jonathan had been about to make:

'I wish I were in Toby's body and Jonathan in Hercules's!'

There was a sudden tingling in Martha's arms and legs and then she felt herself falling forward: she had a distinct sensation of unbalance and uneasiness, of being too high, too thrown back, was glad to feel the grass under her toes as it ought to be, was conscious of running, her legs running almost as if they had a separate life of their own. A warm miasma of smell, of earth and grass enveloped her strongly, and there was something in her mouth; something that writhed and she held firmly, yet delicately, because she knew she shouldn't have it, and so was going to take it to a quiet place she knew to investigate it at her leisure. She had careered on several paces before she realized that the wish had worked and that she was Toby and held Mr Tom between her strong white teeth. She stopped running, and delicately spat Mr Tom out into a rose bed.

'Tom, my dear husband! Are you all right? Did that brute hurt you?'

Mrs Tom, tiny as she was, had come pelting after Toby at a very good pace, leaping pebbles in her path, thrusting her way through high blades of grass.

'I *think* I'm all right,' said Mr Tom rather doubtfully, getting shakily to his feet and brushing himself down.

'Thank goodness for that – for the moment I feared – oh well – I must collect myself – I was about to be quite foolish over you . . . *not* that you're worth it,' and Mrs Tom blew her nose briskly, her moment of human weakness past, and assisted Mr Tom to brush the earth off his blue jacket.

'My pipe,' he said tremulously. 'My pipe . . . I don't seem to have it.'

'Here it is.' She picked it up for him from where it had fallen. 'If you have to have the nasty thing.'

'It'll soothe my nerves. Upon my word, that was an unpleasant experience. What is the dog doing now my dear? What has happened to him? He looks quite different.'

'Martha is inside him now,' replied his wife. 'That was her wish. I hope you enjoy yourself, Martha.'

She gave Martha/Toby an exploratory prod with her umbrella and then turned to escort Mr Tom back up the garden path.

'Lean on me, Tom,' Martha heard her say. 'Take it gently. And don't puff that disgusting smoke into my face, please.'

Martha/Toby meanwhile sat down on the grass and watched them go. Already Martha was conscious of being at a disadvantage; she had no voice, could formulate no words, and there were a dozen things she wanted to ask. But nothing but a little moaning whine came out of her mouth. For instance, where was Toby now – where was her own body – the girl known as Martha? What had happened to Jonathan and Hercules?

'Wuff!' cried Martha/Toby in frustration. 'Wuff! Wuff!'

It was a nice noise to make, though, and she made it again. She found her body (which responded almost of itself) was jumping up and bouncing about the lawn with the force of its barks. She licked her lips; strange, hairy, leathery things they were. She could feel her great teeth with her long tongue. She could lick the end of her nose with her long tongue, how cold and wet it felt! She licked her nose again, then cantered back up the path. How odd, and yet how altogether natural it was to have four legs and to be so near the ground. What a feeling of sturdy stability it gave her. How fast she could move!

Near the rabbit hutch the weather house lay on its side with Mr and Mrs Tom pulling at it to get it the right way up. Martha/Toby had no hands to help, and that was disconcerting, but found she could nudge it with her nose and help them to right it. Mr and Mrs Tom climbed in and disappeared from view.

' . . . a little rest,' she heard Mrs Tom say. 'You'd better have a little rest. Let me arrange the bed. No, you are *not* to smoke in bed, what an idea. Do you want to set the house on fire?'

Meanwhile Martha/Toby's attention was distracted by the sight of a large rabbit lolloping slowly and a little unsteadily towards her. It was obviously Jonathan. Every now and then the rabbit reared up on its back legs and looked about it and twitched its nose and then gave a little jump and frisk; quite unlike Hercules's usual purposeful lope.

And then Martha/Toby saw two figures: the bodies of a ten-year-old girl and boy sitting cross-legged side by side, their backs against the rabbit hutch. Their eyes were shut; their faces blank. They looked more as if they were pretending to be asleep than as if they actually were asleep: as if just enough consciousness were left inside them to keep them sitting there, but not enough for them to move and talk.

It was strangely upsetting to see them.

I didn't know I looked quite like that, thought Martha/Toby, approaching them a little more nearly and sniffing them.

Or smelt like that, she thought next. Goodness, she had had no idea what it was to have a proper nose. Smells, strong, pungent, stirring, exciting, bombarded her from all directions now. She, as Martha, was beginning to sink deeper and deeper into the muscular hairy dog's body. A warm drift of rabbit smell made her wrinkle her nostrils and sniff it up. She had the urgent feeling that she wanted to sink her teeth into it, taste the fur, worry it, crunch the bones, feel the salty taste of blood. What was she thinking of? The rabbit was now Jonathan. How could she think of rending poor Jonathan? She stared at him and sniffed, and he sniffed back and began to scamper round and round in the centre of the lawn in a very un-Hercules manner.

'Wow!' cried Martha in exultation. She bounced and rolled and ran. She drowned in sensation, in the joy of running, the sensation of speed, the richly varied currents of air that blew across the garden, bringing the scent of hens from the cottages across the road, of dinner cooking three doors down, of various birds, of tom-cats. With each sniff she got a different, still more distant aroma to blend with the rich mixture, the symphony of smells in which she was absorbed.

'Wow!' She barked herself round in an ecstatic circle, and now she had discovered her tail. Toby, as part mongrel, part black and white fox terrier, had a lovely long, plumy white tail. What fun it was to have a tail, and to wave it from side to side, screwing oneself round to watch it. It would be fun to try and catch it in her mouth ... Martha made several tries before she tired of it, panting and almost chuckling to herself. But that was one thing dogs couldn't do; laugh. She grinned, letting her tongue fall sideways out of her mouth, and that was the nearest she could get to laughter.

Somewhere in the back of her mind Martha now felt her view of the world changing; she was growing used to seeing everything from the height of about one foot from the ground, but there were other differences. She had no difficulty in recognizing what everything about her *was*; grass, trees, rose bushes, and yet they were altered; the colours dimmer, the shapes less clearly marked. But a thrush, perched on the fence nearby, gleamed out in sharp relief from its background. She could smell it, too. Did she perceive it more clearly than the rose bushes because, as Toby, it was more interesting to her?

She had no more time to think because Jonathan/Hercules ran skittishly up to her and for a short time then both of them entered a mood of almost lunatic gaiety at the strange and heady sensations their new bodies were giving them. They chased one another and jumped over one another and ran and ran. Martha was just in the act of leaping over a big, greenish, vegetable-smelling object which she one half-second later realized to be a cabbage, when she was startled by a hoarse shout, and a clod of earth whistled past her ear.

'Hey! Have the animals gone mad?'

The earth had been thrown by someone they had entirely forgotten; Jonathan's father, who had been sitting quietly in the greenhouse, puffing at his pipe and contemplating his vegetable garden.

They were playing and running now in this vegetable garden, among the early cabbages and lettuces and countless delicate seedlings.

Both Jonathan and Martha, startled from the purely animal pleasure they had been enjoying woke with a great start to the realization of the crime they were committing. They had already done a good deal of damage.

They had no voices with which to apologize, but with one accord they slunk off the vegetable bed into the shelter of the beech hedge which bordered one side of it, quivering with guilt. Martha could feel her tail sinking of its own accord between her back legs. Hidden by the thick hedge they paused together panting, their furry sides heaving in unison.

'Jonathan! Martha!' called Jonathan's father in bewilderment, staring up the lawn towards the house. 'Where are they? How can Hercules be loose like this?'

Knocking out his pipe on the heel of his shoe, he strode off up the lawn, not seeing the seated bodies of his son and son's friend still motionless by Hercules's cage.

Jonathan and Martha had only a few minutes' respite because very soon both Jonathan's parents had come into the vegetable garden to survey the damage.

'Oh, I say, it's too bad,' exclaimed Jonathan's mother. 'Where can the children be to let the animals run about like that? That awful dog of the Grants, he's ruined that entire row of lettuces. I've a good mind to ask the Grants to pay for them. Look, I can see through the gap in the hedge, there's Ruth Grant going down her garden now. Go and tell her about the damage, John.'

'Oh, well, it's all in the day's work. It seems a bit mean to claim for five or six very small lettuces,' said her husband doubtfully. He stood, his hands in his pockets, and made no move, Martha mentally applauding him. She had always liked Jonathan's father a good deal better than his mother. She watched now with a certain amount of interest to see what would happen next.

'Well, if you won't, I will,' announced Jonathan's mother with determination.

From her lair in the beech hedge, Martha watched her go to the gap in the boundary hedge and call out sharply: 'Ruth, Ruth, just a minute, please!'

But what was said next Martha was unable to hear, even with Toby's sharp ears, which she realized were considerably better than her own. She shifted cautiously about within the hedge, quite forgetting her tail, the tip of which protruded out a few inches on one side.

'Get out, you wretch, Toby. Go home!'

The garden broom, a nasty affair of stiff bristles, poked through the leaves to strike her very unpleasantly on her backside.

'Yow!' With a piercing yelp Martha shot out of cover to meet the combined annoyance of the two women: Jonathan's mother on her side of the boundary and her own mother, her face showing through leaves just beyond. Both women called out 'Toby, Toby, bad dog!' in loud shrill voices.

'Toby! Come here this instant,' Ruth Grant called again in peremptory tones and both what was left of Toby the dog and Martha the girl, recognized these tones and hastened meekly to obey. Without consciously knowing there was a hole lower down in the hedge, Martha found herself automatically burrowing through, to emerge in her own garden under her mother's angry eye, and shake herself.

It was a very odd and entirely unpleasant experience, being under that eye not as a wrong-doing girl as had been hitherto the case, but as a bad dog.

'Toby, come here.' Martha/Toby, tail well down, was slinking nearer when Martha suddenly realized what would result from this misdemeanour; Toby was always on such occasions shut in their garden shed for a couple of hours where he would yap indignantly for about half an hour and then go to sleep on a sack in the corner; neither of which things she wanted to do.

So she hastily ran off down to the very bottom of the garden, behind the wood pile and the nettles and the old bit of holly hedge; a place which when she reached it she recognized through Toby's eyes as a good place: it had several old bones there and half a mouldy loaf and a few other bits and pieces which Toby had wished to investigate at leisure and in privacy.

There was silence for a few seconds and then she heard footsteps retreating up the path and presently the back door slammed. What was happening in Jonathan's garden?

She heard the sound of voices, and then Jonathan's mother's voice, very shrill and angry: 'Jonathan, Martha! *Here* you are! Didn't you see what those animals were doing? Jonathan, if this is some silly game you are to stop it immediately!'

A pause. Martha held her breath: what would happen now? Jonathan's mother would surely have hysterics soon if he remained in his present zombie-like condition.

'*Jonathan*!' came his mother's voice again. 'Don't you hear me? What is the matter with you? Oh, I do wish you would take that silly look off your face and answer me!'

And then, almost immediately afterwards, Jonathan's voice came floating over the hedge.

'Sorry, it was just a game. OK, OK, I'll go and capture Hercules.'

Hey, what about me? Martha thought but could not say. She rushed to the hedge and peered through. Yes, there was Jonathan, evidently fully restored to himself, seizing a piece of bread and stalking with a purposeful air after Hercules, who was sitting stockstill in the middle of the lawn, probably very bewildered, but it was difficult to tell from the rabbit's back view what his emotions were.

Poor Martha let out a whine of frustration. There was her body, still sitting by the hutch, ignored by everybody: there was Jonathan, quite restored, there were his parents, both walking back towards their house, the incident over as far as they were concerned. But what about her, Martha? Did Jonathan realize that she was not back in her own body? How had this wish come about? Jonathan's mother had been near the weather house when she made it, was that all it needed? Could she, Martha, ever wish again? And what on earth was Jonathan doing?

She could bear the indecision no longer. Although she was reluctant, as Toby, to set paw in the next door garden for a time, she nevertheless squeezed through the hole in the hedge to communicate her next urgent wish, indeed extremely urgent wish, to Jonathan. She was fed up with being Toby: she wanted to change back, now, immediately.

58

'Ouch!' An exclamation of pain floated across the lawn to her. 'You beast, Hercules, you bit me!' came Jonathan's voice.

Martha could see a sort of flurry of boy and rabbit – then the rabbit dropped to the grass from his master's arms and ran off across the garden, disappearing rapidly from view round the side of the house.

'Hercules!' cried Jonathan vainly. He ran after Hercules, sucking his finger as he went, and soon also had disappeared.

Martha ran up to the body of the ten-year-old girl, still sitting in the same position. It was again strangely unpleasant to see her thus. There was the weather house beside her. Two wooden figures stood near the doors, the man just inside, the woman without. They had obviously had to hide in this fashion: they would wake, that was no problem. Surely it would be no problem?

'Wuff!' Martha barked. 'Wuff!'

She had barked three times before the awful thought struck her. How could she make a wish if she didn't have a voice: couldn't make words?

But the Toms didn't wake up, as she had hoped. Wooden figures they remained and a dog Martha remained: a furry animal with no power of expression, no hands, stuck, power-less in every way that mattered. *Trapped*.

6

The longest ten minutes of Martha's entire life then dragged by. Whimpering with indecision she lay down beside the weather house, occasionally nudging it with her nose, desperately trying to waken its inhabitants and not liking to abandon it. Any minute she expected either one of Jonathan's parents to come out into the garden, but mercifully they did not.

The she heard Jonathan's voice from her garden, and one of the boys, she couldn't tell if it were Paul or Mark, answering him.

'Perhaps he's run off into the field at the back,' she heard. 'He could be anywhere really.'

Wanting to see what was going on she pushed her way back, forgetting the weather house.

She saw Paul and Jonathan walking about the garden, Jonathan looking intensely worried. Then her father appeared. 'What's the matter, Jonathan?' he asked.

'I've lost Hercules,' replied Jonathan in desperate tones. 'He ran right out of our garden onto the road in front, and then a car came along and nearly ran him over and he was scared and ran into your front garden. I know he got into the back garden because your side gate was open and then I lost him.'

'Oh dear,' said Martha's father sympathetically. 'He could be in so many places in this garden, couldn't he? Does he come when he's called?'

'Not really,' replied Jonathan sadly. 'He's not like a dog, you know. And he's frightened.'

'Hallo, Jonathan. Are you in trouble?' Now Mrs Grant was

in the garden too. 'He'll be on our compost heap,' she suggested. 'I've just put some apple peelings down there. Honestly – these *animals* – aren't they a nuisance? Mark's only just recaptured his wretched gerbil. Cheer up, Jonathan, I'm sure we'll find Hercules.'

Yes, but what about *me*? thought Martha frantically to herself. I'm lost too, in a sort of way.

She ran after her parents, Paul and Jonathan, who had moved together towards the compost heap, and was swiftly spotted and shooed back.

'Go away, Toby, bad dog!'

But Martha merely ran in a circle, returning to jump up at Jonathan, barking wildly and taking hold of his jeans in her mouth and tugging at them.

'Stop it, Toby,' he said absently and then to her great relief Martha saw a light of recognition come into his eyes. 'Why Martha – ' he said. 'Oh *golly*. You haven't – *oh*!'

Martha tugged again at his jeans and tried to lead him towards the next door garden. Never, *never* would she wish to be without the power of words again. She tried and tried to form them but Toby's mouth with its long tongue and teeth would only make whines and strange-sounding groans interspersed with the occasional shrill bark.

'Toby: what on earth is the matter?' The Grants stood round looking down in bewilderment.

'I think I've seen Hercules back in my garden,' said Jonathan swiftly. 'And so has Toby – he's trying to tell me – I must go.'

They reached the weather house and Jonathan wished: 'I wish that Martha is restored to her own body.'

The wooden figures stirred into life; and this was the last sight Martha saw with Toby's eyes. She came gently back to her own dear body, feeling its arms and legs with delight. Her hands particularly pleased her and she rubbed them together, appreciating each finger, which moved with such delicate precision wherever she wished it.

'Oh, I'm me! I'm me!' She cried happily, rising to her feet. 'Oh, lovely beautiful me! Oh, isn't it lovely to talk and be me!

Oh, what a gorgeous voice I have, haven't I, Jonathan? Didn't you feel this too when you were changed back?'

'Yes, a bit I suppose,' he answered her glumly. 'But I went back before I was really ready. I was enjoying being Hercules, but oh, Martha, I wish I hadn't done it in a way. Hercules sees things so oddly – I don't know. And I seemed to get some of his memories and he doesn't see me like I thought he did. I thought he loved me in his own sort of way but I don't know that he does at all. I'm just a sort of food getter he knows – Oh, I can't explain. And his body – it's sort of uncertain in some ways. As if he didn't run enough. I wish he'd been a wild rabbit. But then he wouldn't have been *my* rabbit. Oh, Martha, perhaps he *will* go wild now he's lost! But he won't survive, they never do, and it'll be my fault. If only we hadn't had this wish!'

'The consequences of all wishes may be more far-reaching than you know,' said Mrs Tom, solemnly looking at them from the door of the weather house. 'You are often too hasty. But I suppose one can't expect children of your age to have much sense. And now there must be no more wishes for at least three days. Mr Tom needs the rest and so do I after the shock of seeing him in that dog's mouth. Goodbye.'

And she quivered and sank into wood. Mr Tom took up his place behind his door; Mrs Tom remaining just outside.

It may rain soon, thought Martha, looking up at the sky, which was overcast.

At that moment Jonathan's mother called them from the dining-room window.

'Jonathan, lunch is ready.'

'You can come back and lunch with me if you like,' offered Martha.

'No, thank you. Your family doesn't have as good lunches as mine. It's steak and kidney pie today. But, Martha – I'll be round later to look for Hercules again. And do keep an eye out for him, please. He may be hiding somewhere, still very frightened.'

'I'll look out for him,' Martha promised and picked up the weather house and ran back to her own house, followed by

62

Toby, who seemed just the same as ever. He had stretched and yawned at the same time as Martha had delighted in her own recovery of her body, and probably thought he had been asleep.

It had been an extraordinary experience, Martha thought as she went home. She had got a lot nearer to Toby, though she realized that she had only been Toby in one sense of the word. She had looked through his eyes, but she had not thought his thoughts. She had been aware of strange doggy memories, but they had been misty and dreamlike. But unlike Jonathan with Hercules, she was sure that Toby felt anyway some affection for his family and for herself.

'Toby, you do like me, don't you?' She bent and caressed him and he wagged his tail and licked her face. Funny little Toby: she wouldn't shout at him so much in future and drag him about when he didn't feel like it. He was his own person and had his own dignity.

In the hall she met Mark.

'I got Snuffy at last!' he remarked, grinning cheerfully.

'Jolly good.'

Funny old Mark: he was irritating at times but his heart was in the right place.

She went into the kitchen where Paul and her parents were still discussing the whereabouts of Hercules.

Funny old parents and funny old Paul: they really seemed to care. They were all right.

Anna and her boyfriend Steve were in the kitchen too, cutting sandwiches to take out on a picnic.

'Hullo, Martha,' said Anna giving Martha a dazzling, showing-off-in-front-of-boyfriend, smile.

'Hullo.'

Funny old Anna – at least, no. Anna wasn't funny exactly. She was too much the dominating older sister to be funny. But she was nice when she was in a good mood.

'Who's for baked beans and fried eggs?' cried Mrs Grant, brandishing her frying pan. 'That's all that's on offer for lunch unless you want sandwiches. I've had such a broken-up kind of morning, what with animals and things.'

Anna and Steve presently went off with their picnic and the rest of them settled down to feed in the kitchen in a kind of cheerful muddle. Toby pushed a plate of scraps and tinned meat about the floor with the vigour of his hearty gulps and licks and then came and begged at Martha's side. She fed him with crusts of bread and then her father exclaimed: 'There's Hercules, and he's obviously having a good lunch too.'

Hercules's large white body could be plainly seen from the kitchen window moving eagerly about the Grant's vegetable patch. It was smaller and less planned than the one next door so could hardly be dignified with the name 'garden'. As they watched, he settled down to eat a lettuce.

'Better go and fetch Jonathan,' said Mr Grant, smiling at Martha.

'I'll go,' offered Paul. 'I've finished and Martha hasn't.'

So Martha stayed to finish her beans and they all watched Hercules attack his second lettuce.

'We'd only scare him away if we went out,' said her mother. 'I hope Jonathan's quick to come, all the same. Those lettuces took a lot of watering last month, didn't they, darling?'

Martha had a flashback of memory; seeing her parents labour in the garden watering during a dry spell, then earlier, taking turns digging and planting. How different, she suddenly realized, from Jonathan's parents. His mother never worked in the garden: that was his father's job. How boring always to be inside a house!

Mrs Grant was laughing now as they watched Hercules. 'This seems to me to sort of even things up with next door,' she said. 'Toby runs over their veg garden and Hercules eats ours. But I shan't go bustling round complaining to Irene.'

'Still, it would be nice if Irene knew.'

'What I might do is sort of slip it in and then laugh it off as if I didn't mind (which I don't). I shall just say to Irene how glad we are that Hercules hasn't met a sticky end and say how he enjoyed himself in our vegetables, dear thing, something like that.'

'She'll probably either not notice, or else think you an even bigger fool that she thought you before, for not caring,' said her husband sagely.

'There's Jonathan,' cried Martha in relief. 'And he's holding Hercules. Thank goodness for that!'

'And I've got Snuffy,' said Mark. 'So it's all ended well, hasn't it?'

'Yes,' echoed Martha, caressing Toby behind the ears, where he particularly appreciated it. 'All's well that ends well. It's nice to be us, isn't it?'

But although her family smiled and agreed with her, none of them understood to the full what she had meant.

7

'The Toms are awake again,' said Martha to Jonathan. 'It's three days now.'

It was late on Tuesday afternoon, after school and tea. They were in Jonathan's room, because Jonathan was very absorbed in building a model aeroplane there and did not want to leave it.

'Mmn,' said Jonathan absently, staring at a part of the undercarriage.

'So we can begin to think about what we want next,' continued Martha, walking about his neat room and fiddling with the collection of little cars on his window sill.

'Do you mind,' he said, looking up. 'That Bugatti comes at the end, not halfway down the line.'

'And we have five more wishes,' continued Martha, obediently putting the car in its rightful place. 'The one made by your mother didn't count. Mr and Mrs Tom had quite an argument about it.'

'Oh?'

'I asked them, you see, and at first Mrs Tom said a wish was a wish whoever made it; after all, she'd had to make the effort granting it, but then Mr Tom said she was to remember that we had saved his life, and hadn't had time to think out the wording of my wish properly, and so it had needed an extra wish to get back again, and they shouldn't count *that*. Anyway – after a lot of argument he got her to agree that although three wishes were used up last Saturday, they would only reckon it as one. So we have five more. I think that was nice of Mr Tom, don't you? I *did* think she was the fairest really, but I'm not so sure now. I thought he was too dreamy to care about us; but he isn't always. He was quite sharp with her and told her she should be more generous-minded. And she gave him a look and just shut up.'

'Yeah,' said Jonathan, drawing the word out, deeply absorbed again in his aeroplane.

'Oh, Jonathan! I do wish you'd pay a bit more attention,' remarked Martha irritably. 'I want to know what you want to do next. We must think it out carefully. They're beginning to run out and I want to be invisible and I want to go back in Time (or forward if you prefer) and I want to do all sorts of things, so come on, do stop working on that aeroplane and think!'

Silence. Jonathan carefully fitted a wing into place.

'Jonathan!'

'I *am* thinking. And I don't know about another wish just yet. I didn't like the last one.'

'But it ended all right. It was horrible losing Hercules like that, but you got him back again.'

'Yes, but as I told you, I wish I hadn't had that wish. I don't feel the same about Hercules, and though he's used to being in that cage a lot I think he should have more runs than I can give him. But if I let him loose in the garden I'm told off. I wish you could put a lead on a rabbit and take it for a walk,' he ended gloomily.

'I'm sorry, Jonathan. I really am. But *do* let's think about the next wish now.'

'I don't want to, not yet anyway,' he muttered, puzzling over the blueprint for making the aeroplane. 'Oh, blast these stupid instructions. They don't make sense.'

'Oh, you don't make sense, Jonathan!' exclaimed Martha angrily. She suddenly felt extremely irritable, and felt Jonathan was deliberately making it worse. It had been a horrible day altogether, grey, cold weather with a spiteful wind tearing at the roses and blowing dust in one's eyes. Then Martha had been told she hadn't been working hard enough at her arithmetic when in fact she'd been absolutely busting herself over her fractions. Arithmetic was the most terrible subject for getting one into a temper, too. So she had come home all upset to find a row going on between Anna and her mother. Anna had said that she didn't want to be a part of the family holiday in August: she had it all planned out and was going camping with Steve in the Lake District.

'Oh no, you're not,' countered her mother swiftly. 'Not if it's just the two of you, you're not.'

'Anna, don't you *want* to come to Cornwall with us?' Martha had cried out, deeply wounded. 'We had such fun last year, don't you remember?'

'Oh, Martha, don't you start on me,' flashed Anna tensely. 'These family holidays are all very well for you, but don't you see they *bore* me?'

'I thought you enjoyed it,' Martha had wept. For some reason these words of Anna's had cut her to the heart; she felt they were a betrayal of the family as such, and she felt angry and sorry on her mother's behalf as well. How could Anna be so hurtful?

But her mother, though a little upset, had not been as devastated as Martha would have expected of her.

'You can make your own holiday arrangements if you like,' she said steadily. 'But I'd prefer you to be in a group of young people, not all alone with your boyfriend at your age.'

'Oh, *Mummy*,' wailed Anna and then Martha had left them to it. She thought for a few moments of wishing for a good holiday for the whole family, but that was so far ahead, and it was at this point that she felt that another wish, any other wish would break this unpleasant day and put her in a better mood, and so she had called on Jonathan. And now *he* was letting her down.

'If you don't look out I shall have a wish all by myself, then,' she cried.

'You can if you like, I don't care,' he replied coldly. 'Where's the other blooming strut then? I shall have to get Dad to help me on this one . . .'

At this point Martha's temper, never her strong point, overboiled.

'All right, it would serve you right if I had *all* the other wishes to myself,' she cried. 'As for your silly plane I hope you bust it! I hope it never flies! I hope your Dad never helps you. You are the most irritating boy! And as for your Mum and your Dad I think they're simply silly – all my family think so too – they laugh at them like anything, my family do!'

It was unforgiveable. Some boys might not have minded rude things said about their parents, but Jonathan was not among their number and Martha, if she had not been lashing out so wildly, should have known this. He raised his head and looked at her and she could tell from his expression how she had wounded him.

'All right, if you feel like that about us, you can get out of this house,' he said icily. 'Have your stupid wishes and don't come back, see?'

Martha instantly realized what she had done, and was stricken to the heart. How could she unsay those words? She would have liked to tear out her stupid tongue.

'I'm sorry. I didn't mean . . .' she stammered. 'I didn't mean it, Jonathan.'

'Oh, yes you did.' He faced her, implacable. 'Go away, can't you? I don't want you.'

'Oh!' Martha looked at him for a moment more and then, realizing it was useless, turned and ran blindly out of the house, tears streaming down her face.

She reached her own house, raced upstairs and collapsed on her bed her fists on the pillow and sobbing to herself. 'Oh, oh, oh, I wish I hadn't said it, I wish I hadn't said it!'

'Said what, for heaven's sake?' enquired a sharp little voice, just by her pillow. Martha raised tear-dimmed eyes to see that both the Toms had somehow climbed her counterpane to stare at her inquisitively.

'Poor old Martha,' said Mr Tom gently. 'But we can't give you a wish with such a vague wording as that now, can we?'

'You must be more explicit,' put in Mrs Tom, not unsympathetically.

Martha's sobs subsided and she sat up slowly. 'Do you mean you *can* help?' she said. 'I hadn't thought you might . . . If only I hadn't said those awful things to Jonathan! If something is once said, how can one possibly unsay it?'

'Actually that *is* a bit tricky,' mused Mr Tom, climbing up on her pillow and sitting there reflectively. 'Time wishes have very strong laws bound up in them, you see.'

'I was going to have a wish going back in Time,' sniffed Martha. 'If Jonathan had wanted it too, that is. But now he says he doesn't want to have anything more to do with me.'

'We couldn't have given you a very satisfactory Time wish, anyway,' said Mrs Tom, pacing up and down on Martha's counterpane. 'Nothing must happen in a Time wish that alters the future events by one jot, you must see that. Therefore you can go back and watch but only as a kind of ghost. You can't speak to anyone, and you can't displace one single atom. Otherwise the whole Future might be affected. It could cause terrible rents in the whole fabric of Time.'

'What did you say to Jonathan?' asked Mr Tom thoughtfully. 'And how long ago was it?'

Martha told him, tears beginning to well again in her eyes as she realized the unalterableness of what she had done.

'Did you speak to or see anyone else but Jonathan?' persisted Mr Tom thoughtfully.

'No. And I ran straight back here.'

'So it was just a period of about ten minutes confined entirely to Jonathan and yourself?'

'Yes,' said Martha, beginning to have the faintest glimmer of hope.

'What do you say, my dear?' He turned to his wife. 'I think it might be almost possible, considering the boy is already used to magic – I can't see it would do any harm. And it was so very recently that Time has hardly had time to settle in any major way – '

'No – ,' she said slowly. 'Let me think. This is dangerous work. As every second ticks by it gets more dangerous. We can't do it so easily if, for instance, Jonathan has already gone into the kitchen and told his mother all about the quarrel . . .'

'The sooner the better, then.' Mr Tom jumped off the pillow, as brisk and alert as Martha had ever seen him. 'You are agreed, Martha? This is to be your Time wish? You wish to relive the last ten minutes or quarter of an hour (I can break you in at exactly the right moment, so don't worry about how many minutes it actually is). You wish to relive it so you can act in a different manner and not say the bad things you did?'

'Yes! Yes!' cried Martha eagerly. 'Please, please may I do that?'

'Your fifth wish is granted,' said Mr and Mrs Tom then, both together.

There was a whirling sensation, as if she were taken from behind and drawn rapidly backwards and Martha found herself in Jonathan's room again.

'If you don't look out, I shall have a wish all by myself then,' she was exclaiming. This time she could hear the cross, scratchy note in her voice and realized the way it affected Jonathan, and understand his ill humour too, because his aeroplane was not going right.

'You can if you like, I don't care. Where's the other blooming strut then? I shall have to get Dad to help me with this one . . .'

Although Martha was on her guard this time she could feel the temper rising in her in just the same way. But this time she clenched her hands together and even brought them up to her mouth in order to check the words that wanted to burst out of her. But already, just by making this movement she had done something different and this heartened her. She did not trust herself to speak but turned her back on Jonathan and went and stared out of the window down his garden and fixed her mind on an enormous blackbird tugging a worm from a flowerbed, heaving away at it, its legs set firmly apart for a good balance. How unpleasant it must be to be a worm. Suddenly it was gobbled up and Martha began to feel a good deal better. Now she could say something different, to take herself and Jonathan on a new tack.

'OK,' she said slowly, 'I may have just one more wish on my own. It's not a very exciting one, but it's something I have to do. And then we'll have one together later on, when you feel more like it. I'm sure we can think of something good. After all, it was fun flying, wasn't it?'

He raised his head from his aeroplane and looked at her then. 'It was super,' he said quietly. 'That's why I want this aeroplane to work, it will sort of remind me.'

'I expect your Dad will get it right for you,' said Martha.

'Yes, he always helps if I want him to, but I'd rather have done it on my own. Why don't you go home, Martha? Dad'll be in soon and then it'll be supper time.'

'OK,' Martha said peacefully. Jonathan's voice had been dismissive, but not cross.

'We'll have another wish tomorrow or the day after, whenever you like,' she continued.

'Yes.' He was turning back to the plane when there was the sound of the front door banging.

'Dad!'

Footsteps came up the stairs, and Martha was expecting Jonathan's father to come in, but then there was the oddest pause: Jonathan stayed in the same position looking towards his open bedroom door, the sounds outside ceased, and Martha was momentarily conscious of physical movement being arrested; she tried to move towards the door and for an instant could not. This strange pause lasted perhaps three seconds and then time flowed again. Martha made the step she had been intending to make towards the door, and Jonathan's father came in, in his neat blue suit.

'Hullo, Martha!' he said heartily.

'Hullo,' replied Martha. 'At least – goodbye. I've got to go now. Goodbye, Jonathan.'

''Bye,' he replied absently and as Martha went out she could hear him eagerly explaining his problem to his father.

Martha breathed a great sigh of relief and returned to her own house and bedroom, where she found the Toms sitting together on her bed.

'Did you notice the three-second repair?' asked Mr Tom. 'We're quite proud of that; it was the only little problem we had.'

'You mean just before Jonathan's Dad came in?'

'Yes. You see, that was the only divergence which didn't concern just the two of you. What had originally happened was that his father had come home, Jonathan had called him in much the same way, he had gone upstairs and into Jonathan's room and then been struck by Jonathan's look of sadness; his eyes were full of tears, and he's not a boy to cry easily. So his father had said to him, "What's the matter, old boy?" and Jonathan was just going to reply when we broke in and sent them ten minutes back in time. Apart from that, and you were the only one to know about it, everything has fitted in very neatly.'

'There was a slight elongation of time while you were looking at the blackbird – just to fill in a bit, but that was such a simple matter I don't expect you noticed,' remarked Mrs Tom.

'No,' said Martha. 'And thank you very, very much. We were both in bad moods, I understand that now. Oh goodness, I feel so much better! It's such a relief not to have quarrelled.'

'Yes. A good neat job of work,' said Mrs Tom with satisfaction, standing up and smoothing her dress.

'You see, we *can* work together very well still when we try,' said her husband also rising to his feet, and his hand lingered for a moment near the lower regions of his wife's back and he gave her the slightest pat somewhere below the belt of her blue dress.

'Tch, tch,' said Mrs Tom, knocking his hand away. But she was smiling. It made her face look quite different.

However, the Time wish was not completely over. The next afternoon Jonathan walked back with Martha from school and stayed for tea, as his mother had a hairdressing appointment. After tea they went up to Martha's room, both of them in a much more relaxed mood than that of the previous afternoon.

The weather was still cloudy, but the cold wind had dropped and it was still and calm: a boring, colourless yet peaceful day. School had been boring and peaceful too; they had had Art all afternoon.

Martha lay on her bed flat on her back, occasionally

meditatively raising her legs both together in the air as if she were doing some tummy-reducing exercise. Jonathan sat on her window sill, kicking his heels against the wall beneath and whistling. Mr Tom sat astride the roof of the weather house cleaning out his pipe while Mrs Tom, a handkerchief about her head, was bustling in and out, dusting. She even dusted the book on which the house was sitting.

'Anna gave me some paint,' said Martha, suddenly remembering. 'Green paint! I didn't know if you'd like it or not. It's under my bed, along with one or two other things. I was going to paint your house.'

'Oh. Let me see.'

Mrs Tom energetically pulled it out into the middle of the room. It was only a very small pot, but it was barrel-sized for her.

'Hmn. Emerald,' she said. 'I think it might make me sneeze.'

'It looks good,' said Mr Tom peering down. 'I'd like to have a go with that.'

'I daresay you would,' she replied tartly. 'No, I think not, Martha. I think we'll stay as we are for the time being.'

Mr Tom shrugged his shoulders. 'As you will, my dear. But it would be nice to be smart.'

'Ah, we *were* smart once, in the old days. And look at the pickle we're in now.'

'It's no good repining,' he said.

'I know. But when I think of my kitchen and how I had everything sparkling and arranged just as I wanted it – all my jars and conserves and pots and pans – and the living room, my brasses and silver and the garden – I can't help feeling sad.'

'You had a garden?' Martha asked.

'We had a garden.' Mrs Tom fell silent.

'I suppose wishing yourselves back in Time wouldn't do any good?' asked Martha sympathetically. 'So you could have it all as it used to be?'

'No. I thought I'd explained – we can't make any wishes for ourselves. Anyway in our case the passage of Time is far too

74

great: we made a mess of things and we have to bear the consequences,' said Mrs Tom in a matter-of-fact voice. 'I suppose we could go back for a little while just as spectators – ghosts – and watch the picture of ourselves as we used to be, but I don't want to do that. It would be far too painful, wouldn't it, Mr T?'

'Yes,' he said shortly.

'What *did* you do wrong?' burst in Jonathan curiously. 'Are you ever going to tell us? I suppose you'd have to tell us if we wished it.'

'We'll tell you in our own good time, but not now,' said Mrs Tom briskly. 'You won't have to wish it. And about going back and looking – that's a very simple thing you know. In fact, you've given me an idea. Martha's last wish was a small, though intricate, affair and Jonathan missed out on it altogether. I think I could throw in a straightforward Grade C Time wish with it, as part of your fifth wish without any trouble at all.'

'What was Martha's wish?' asked Jonathan.

'How do you mean?' asked Martha, and they both spoke together.

'Martha's wish was private, to undo something she regretted,' Mrs Tom told him, 'and what I mean for now is that I can, if you like, take you back any amount of years you wish, just for a short look. If you're interested, that is.'

'Yes!' cried Jonathan. 'Could we see the Battle of Trafalgar – something like that?'

'No – that's a Grade B at least. A lot more effort. What I can do for you most easily and it isn't so much, so don't get excited, is not a mixture of Time and Place which is always more complicated, but a simple Time wish in *this* place.'

'You mean in this house?' asked Martha. 'It isn't as old as all that, though it's older than Jonathan's. Anna remembers Jonathan's being built: before that it was just an orchard belonging to another house further down.'

'You could go back to any date you liked in this house, of course,' said Mrs Tom. 'But that would only take you back to 1910, or thereabouts. The *land* on which this house has been built is nearly as old as this world, of course, many hundreds of millions of years. And there have been countless houses, huts and shelters of one kind or another here. It's a good site: sheltered by the wood and the rising hills on one side and water easily available under the ground just a few paces away. The road has been a road of some kind leading up to the hills for about ten thousand years. I expect there's been something or other happening around here for a goodish time.'

'Anybody fighting?' asked Jonathan. 'Any battles?'

'No battles just here – though it would be a different matter in the wood, or up in the hills. There'd be a few scuffles, I expect. People walloping each other.'

'I don't want to see that particularly,' said Martha doubtfully. 'Could we go back to a time when there were children of our age here, and see them do something interesting?'

'All right,' said Mrs Tom graciously. 'Just give me a moment to run it over in my mind and see the sort of thing . . . Ah, yes. I should think this would do. Shall I speak the wish for you – it has to be spoken – and Martha will repeat it after me.'

'We wish to go back for a period lasting about half an hour and watch the events taking place here precisely three hundred and one years, eleven hours and – let me see – fourteen and a half minutes ago.'

Martha obediently repeated the wish and almost immediately they found themselves not in a house but standing outside on the cobblestones of a farmyard. The farm house, of timber, lath and plaster, was a small one and surrounded by various outbuildings, stables and barns. Three separate piles of dung stood steaming gently in various places in the yard and were picked over by a collection of scraggy looking red hens. It was quite the dirtiest, muckiest farmyard Martha and Jonathan had ever seen, with mud and straw scattered all about it, and rotting pieces of wood, old wheels with nettles growing over them, and scattered pieces of sacking and hide ground deep into the manure and mud. A dog lay outside a kennel gnawing at an enormous bone. Its eyes looked at them for a moment and Martha saw the hackles rise along its neck and back, and then it turned back to the bone.

'This isn't the right place, it can't be,' said Jonathan, confused. 'There aren't *any* other houses. And the wood comes right round to the back, look.'

'There's the church,' cried Martha, pointing in the direction of the village green. 'You can just see it in exactly the same way as you can from our front gate. And there wouldn't be any other houses – all our road must have been built at different times much less than three hundred years ago. I can see some cottages by the church, can't you? Look at the smoke.'

And she pointed over what should have been a meandering row of houses and gardens and was now a large field with black and white cows to what was obviously the old part of the village.

'There are still cottages on the other side of the road,' exclaimed Jonathan. 'Only they are quite different.'

There were several wooden, thatched hovels, very small and all set higgledy-piggledy about a patch of rough ground with gorse bushes on it. Clothes were drying on the bushes and there were some goats tethered.

'Nothing special seems to be happening here,' said Martha, turning back towards the farm house. It was odd, finding it all so altered. She had expected it to be different, of course, but not quite so different as this, not so that she would be uncertain as to directions – for she could not make out in her mind exactly *where* in her nowadays garden this farmhouse was. They walked round the yard, exploring, and came upon a pond, and a well, but these were no help at all, for they certainly did not exist in the twentieth century.

'I wonder where all the water went,' said Martha, looking at the little pond, bright green with scum, and at the few ducks on it. 'And what is going to *happen*?'

They held their breath and waited. Nobody seemed to be about except the dog and the hens. The occasional thud from a horse's hoof within the stables proved that other animals were near at hand. The sun was setting behind the trees and there were long shadows. The dung heaps continued to steam gently and give out a very penetrating smell in the warm evening air.

Then there was a sudden shout from within the farm house. Silence again. The dog pricked his ears.

'Look,' said Jonathan. 'There's smoke coming out of that window there.' He pointed at the grey wisp drifting out and it thickened as they looked. There was a confused hubbub of voices within the house now, and another noise, a stealthy hissing, a crackling.

'Fire!' exclaimed Jonathan. 'The house is on fire!'

'We must tell them,' cried Martha, quite forgetting how impossible this would be.

But hardly had she taken a step towards the house when a youngish man in his shirt sleeves and with breeches ending at his knee and dirty woollen stockings without boots came running out of the front door with a bucket in his hand.

'Oh lord save us!' he was shouting. 'Fire! Oh lord protect us! Fire!'

He blundered towards the pond, frightening a few ducks off it in a great squawking flurry, and, dipping the bucket into the scummy water, raced back with it towards the house. Flames were now appearing amongst the smoke, and he collided at the doorway with other people running out, all shouting and bawling 'Fire! Fire!'

The other people were an old man clutching a knife and a wooden plate, a youth of about seventeen with a pewter tankard in one hand and a box under his arm, and two women, both youngish with long, untidy hair, clutching shawls about their shoulders, one with a young baby in her arms.

''Tis burning merrily,' one of them cried. 'We'd best get everything out.'

'The childer!' suddenly the other screamed. 'Where's my children!'

And then Martha and Jonathan saw a boy and girl, obviously a brother and sister very near in age come running out of the door together. They were good-looking, fair-haired, healthy children who seemed to have their wits about them better than the grown-ups who were wailing and wringing their hands and doing very little in the way of fire fighting activities.

The girl, about Martha's age, was clutching a large Tabby cat, which added its squalls to the general clamour. The boy was dragging an oak chest after him.

'There's your cloth and linen saved, mother,' he said to one of the women. But she hardly looked at it. 'Where's the little 'un?' she suddenly broke out crying. 'Little Johnny, where's he?'

They all turned to look, and call his name but there was no reply. Flames were roaring now out of the window and smoke beginning to curl from the oaken door, flung right back on its hinges.

'I see him!' Martha yelled. She could see a little white face pressed against one of the upstairs windows which were very small in size and with little diamond-shaped panes of glass.

But nobody else seemed to have noticed the child. The man with the bucket went on throwing water in a wild sort of way at the flames, a good deal of it missing them altogether, while the youth ran round the back of the house, where there was a great whinnying from the horses in the stables who had smelled the smoke.

The women went as far as the hallway of the house, peering into the blazing kitchen and screaming and sobbing: 'Christ in heaven, was he within? Did'st see the little lad within?'

'Nay, I know not: oh, pray that he's not burning to a cinder, the poor little fellow!'

'Upstairs!' Martha shrieked at them, pulling at their long bedraggled skirts, but they took no notice of her, and indeed she found she could make no impression on the material or their bodies at all, her hands simply encountered air. Air that was becoming increasingly murky and hot.

Meanwhile Jonathan, also shouting vainly, was running up the bare wooden staircase that led to four bedrooms at the top of the house. Martha stopped her useless pulling at the women, for she saw both the girl and the boy also running upstairs.

'This way,' called Jonathan from the right bedroom, but the girl, who had reached the top of the stairs first, had turned the wrong way, crying, 'John, Johnny, don't play hide and seek now . . .'

The boy turned in Jonathan's direction, but entered the room to the right of the staircase, over the kitchen, only for a minute and then, to Martha's anguish, ran out of it again. She ran in herself, to see Jonathan bending over a very little boy in the corner beyond the big bed.

'He didn't see him, he was hiding under the bed,' Jonathan said to Martha. 'He seems quite all right, but it's getting very hot in here.'

The air was dark and thick. Both Martha and Jonathan began to cough and so did the two-year-old, for that was all he was. He was naked from the waist down, clad only in a shirt and little waistcoat and he sat on the floor sucking a dirty thumb, his nose running and his eyes streaming. But he made no sound. And it was quite evident that he could see neither Martha nor Jonathan, nor could they make him, or anybody else, hear them. He was crouched half under the bed, and was partly covered by the grimy red woollen curtain that was drawn about the bed, which was a four-poster.

'Oh, get up!' Martha willed. him, after vainly trying to haul him to his feet. 'Please get up!'

The toddler looked through her and did the next best thing; he set up a wail, which ended in a coughing fit.

'Johnny!'

The older brother was back, flushed and desperate.

'Here you are, you scoundrel!' and to Martha and Jonathan's intense relief he struggled with the fat toddler, who was no lightweight, and picked him up somehow and stumbled, coughing, to the top of the stairs where his sister waited for him. Together the two children somehow got the little boy down the stairs, closely followed by Martha and Jonathan.

It was very hot in the hall now and flames were licking into it from one side.

They all fell out into the blessed cool air together, the toddler now kicking and screaming lustily but firmly grasped, upside down, by his older brother.

Martha and Jonathan felt as choked and hot and exhausted as the other children and sat as they did on the dirty cobble-stones and sobbed and coughed.

Through the smoke and confusion Martha could see more people run up from the nearby cottages, with more buckets of water and with brooms for beating the fire and shovels of earth for throwing on it. Many more things were being dragged out from within; an oak table, a settle, some chairs, pots, pans and earthenware, jugs and a few pieces of china.

There was nothing that looked as if it had much value, but everything was set in the muddy farmyard which grew more and more crowded.

'Do you mind?' said Jonathan bitterly to a great red-faced woman, who had just walked blindly through him carrying out a tub full of clothes.

'Let's get out of the way,' said Martha, recovering herself somewhat and scrambling to her feet. 'It's not nice being walked into, is it?'

So they retreated to the door of the barn, and watched the fire being put out. Slowly the flames lessened and gave way to more and more smoke, and the end of the house which had been on fire began to emerge as a blackened filthy shell. The floor of the room above the kitchen didn't cave in, and the fire had never reached the other side of the house. But a good deal of damage had evidently been done – and oh, the mess!

'Poor people,' said Jonathan, watching them as they began to try and appraise the damage.

'What's to do, what's to do?' the old man wailed constantly.

'Hold thy peace, old 'un, 'tis no fault of thine. We'll beg our cousins' aid: they'll help us,' Martha heard one of the women say. 'George, you'd best send word.' She turned to the man who had had the bucket. 'The children and I at least will lodge at their house this night. I care not to lay my head on a smoke-filled blackened pillow. I take Beth and the old man with me. You men can shift for yourselves – it's your lack of care started this blaze.'

'Hold your tongue,' he grumbled in a weary, dispirited voice. 'Women are good for nothing but blaming others.'

'Don't they have cause, then?' she turned on him shrilly, and others joined in, in a babel of voices.

'I think I've seen all I want to see –' Jonathan was beginning when the scene before their eyes began to move and shake as if it were melting and the fire had got at it and they found themselves back in Martha's room.

'You see what I mean about not being able to alter things,' said Mrs Tom to them. 'Though in fact there would not have been much you could have done there, anyway. The child was saved by his brother, as you saw.'

'It was horrid all the same,' shuddered Martha. 'Even if nobody was hurt. But their poor house was all spoilt and they weren't rich people, were they?'

'No, but they looked and were poorer than they needed to be,' said Mrs Tom severely. 'They were a feckless, shiftless family and the fire was entirely their own fault.'

'What happened to them after the fire?' asked Jonathan. 'Did they rebuild that bit of the house and go on living there?'

'Yes, eventually. After they had sponged on their richer cousins in the next farm down the valley for a time and borrowed money which they never repaid – yes – they rebuilt and indeed built on a bit more at the same time and the family went on living there for several further generations. Eventually, through neglect, it fell into ruin and the land lay fallow until the last stones were pulled down and your house was built, Martha.'

'Oh,' said Martha, thinking about it.

'What happened to that boy who saved his brother?' asked Jonathan. 'I liked him.'

'Same as most people. He grew up, married, had children, inherited the farm, ran it no better and no worse than his father and died in his fifties of a stroke.'

'Oh,' said Jonathan, a little disappointed.

'And the girl?' asked Martha.

'Died of the typhus fever a couple of years after the fire.'

'Oh.' Now it was Martha's turn to be disappointed. 'What a shame. And the little boy they rescued. What happened to him?'

'Now he did have a rather different life, that one,' said Mrs Tom, in a musing tone of voice, as if she had known him, and was remembering.

'He enlisted as a soldier under Marlborough and was killed at the Battle of Blenheim, fighting very bravely.'

'Oh.'

That sounded a little better; but it was also somehow unsatisfactory. 'Didn't any of the people living round about do anything else exciting?' asked Jonathan.

'No,' said Mrs Tom briskly. 'They just grew up, married, had children, died – and worked; some hard, some not so hard.'

'Rather boring really,' said Martha. 'Their lives don't seem to amount to anything very much, said like that.'

'*Most* people's lives don't amount to anything very much,' Mrs Tom said. 'Seen from the outside, that is.'

'Ah, but seen from the inside, by the people living them, that's a different matter,' put in Mr Tom, smiling at Martha.

'I think Time is very odd indeed – ' Martha was beginning reflectively when Jonathan startled her by jumping heavily off the window sill.

'Do you hear the church clock striking seven?' he cried. 'I must go.'

Martha lingered for a few more minutes in her room before going downstairs. There was a lot she wanted to say, but she couldn't think of the right words for it.

The journey back to the past had affected her in some way which would have been hard to describe: it had made tears come to her eyes, but that was not just because she felt sorry for the people who had burnt part of their house. It was in some way the same kind of emotion she felt watching sheep being herded in the fields, or calves loaded into a lorry, or little dogs yanked along behind people's feet in crowded thoroughfares. Was it that the sheep and calves and dogs had the same kind of bewildered incomprehension in their faces: "Oh, what is happening to me? Where am I being taken?" Did the people she had just seen have something of this look too? Where was Time taking them? Where was Time taking *her*?

The house martins, who built nests in the eaves of the house, were in the middle of their evening dance, swooping up and down, steering their usual course round the big apple tree. She stared at them, only half seeing them.

'Time is . . . Life is . . . Oh, *why*?' she got out eventually.

'I'm inclined to agree with you,' said Mrs Tom drily. 'It *is*, isn't it? And I don't altogether know why, either.'

8

'Martha!' called her mother the next afternoon when Martha came home from school.

'Yes?' Martha called back, feeling instantly guilty. What mess had she made of her room now? From the efficient tone of her mother's voice and the collection of Hoover, dustpan and brush and dusters on the top of the stairs, it was not difficult to conclude that the bedrooms were being turned out.

'I've been having such a good go at your bedroom,' said her mother brightly, coming out of it. 'As it's Wednesday afternoon and my free-from-school day, I thought I'd do some long overdue housework upstairs – I mean really getting under the beds instead of just a lick and promise, and darling, I was *so* touched when I had everything out from under your bed.'

'Huh?' said Martha, bewildered. Such was not her mother's usual reaction when she had been spending time getting everything out from under Martha's bed.

'I don't mean that there wasn't the usual frightful mess,' continued her mother. 'I mean like a pot of paint under there – that's *not* the right place to keep a pot of paint – but I found something else too and it really was most sweet and generous of you. Where did you get the money for it, though? That's what beats me.'

'You mean Daddy's picture,' said Martha, illumination breaking through.

'Yes. You bought it at the fête, didn't you? It was a lovely idea, and gave him such pleasure, to think he'd sold something. But how did you afford it? Did you combine with Anna and the boys?'

'No,' said Martha, trying to think quickly. 'But I did have some money – you see I kind of did a job for somebody.'

'Who?' asked her mother, with her usual unerring sense for awkward questions.

'I promised I wouldn't tell. It really is all right – I didn't steal any or anything . . .' floundered Martha, feeling herself turning beet red, as if she had come by the money illegally.

'This job, it truly wasn't anything you shouldn't have done? The pay seems very high,' commented Mrs Grant, a little uneasily.

'No, no. I sort of added bits of money I'd saved together – and Jonathan too. He helped me buy it,' remembered Martha with relief.

'Oh, I see. I won't inquire further if you don't want me to. But it was awfully nice of you and Jonathan.'

'We were going to give it away – to – someone who will be sure to like it,' continued Martha quickly. 'But we haven't thought who yet.'

'All right, darling; perhaps it had better not stay in your room too long. Perhaps I can help you think of someone who might like it and who wouldn't spill the beans to Daddy. Leave it to me.'

And with that Mrs Grant seemed to be quite satisfied and humming gently to herself she descended the staircase laden with the Hoover, the dustpan and the dusters and went into the kitchen to put the kettle on.

Later on Martha heard her on the telephone in the hall chatting to one of her friends and was embarrassed all over again to hear her mother's voice brightly exclaiming: 'Yes, I really was proud of Martha. She can be such a sweet child when she tries.'

Ugh! *Must* her mother discuss her more or less in her presence? Why did mothers have to have such long, loud conversations with their women friends, telling all these shaming things about one, as if one was deaf, or invisible or something . . .

Invisible! This was not the first time the idea had come to Martha, but now it struck her with renewed force that to be invisible, say for the space of one day, certainly no more, might be a lot of fun. But she didn't want to do it if Jonathan wasn't keen. If he was, they could both be invisible together. There were many interesting possibilities. Should they be invisible at home or at school? On the whole Martha favoured the idea of school. She resolved to ask Jonathan's opinion without any more ado.

'Oh, school, it's got to be school,' cried Jonathan eagerly, some five minutes later, his eyes glistening with anticipation. 'I can think of some fabulous things to do at school, can't you? We can really baffle the teachers! And there's a games period tomorrow morning too. That should be great. But, Martha, let's just make it for the morning. I want to be visible to eat my school dinner. Perhaps one can't eat at all when one's invisible, or they'd see the food going down inside one. That wouldn't be very nice.'

'The only thing is, people will wonder where we've come from if we suddenly appear at dinner time, not having been there, as they think, in the morning.'

'Oh, we could have been to the dentist, or something,' exclaimed Jonathan, brushing Martha's objections aside. 'I'll say my mum took us both to the dentist as we both had appointments and it took us just about all morning, waiting for one another. Dentists can take ages, anyway.'

'All right. That's not a bad idea. Jonathan, you'd better come round to my house quite early, hadn't you? So we can make the wish together before school time.'

'OK, I'll be round by eight o'clock,' he promised eagerly.

'. . . and we want to be visible again by lunchtime,' finished Martha carefully.

'Very well, my dear, so you will be,' agreed Mr Tom.

'Just a minute, Mr T, I foresee a little difficulty,' put in Mrs Tom. 'Invisibility is easy enough, but if Jonathan and Martha are going to the school all morning, how can we oversee them? They can't carry us in their invisible hands, now can they?'

'I hadn't thought of that!' exclaimed Martha blankly. 'Can't you be invisible too?'

'That would be much more difficult – and there's the

problem of our house, too. We can't alter our house,' said Mr Tom, shaking his head doubtfully.

'Do we really need you anyway?' asked Jonathan. 'We've made such a careful wish I don't see how it could go wrong. And it'll be over by lunch time.'

'No, put that way I don't expect you do need us,' agreed Mr Tom, giving a great yawn. 'Heigho, I'm uncommonly sleepy this morning. The owls kept me awake in the night, telling each other where the good hunting was.'

'It's always advisable, having us near at hand.' Mrs Tom still looked doubtful. 'However – if that's the way you want it. Remember whatever happens you won't be able to make another wish – you'll be too far away, right outside the stipulated boundaries.'

Martha and Jonathan looked at each other.

'We'll just have to risk that,' said Jonathan firmly.

'Very well, wish number six granted,' cried Mrs Tom, writing away in her notebook.

There was a few seconds silence. Then, 'Where am I?' said Martha blankly, looking down at nothing.

It was a ridiculous thing to say, considering that she had known perfectly well what was going to happen, but it was extremely odd to say the very least to feel oneself standing by the window in one's bedroom but not to see one's feet in socks and sandals on the bedroom carpet as they should have been. For a moment she lost balance, took an uncertain step, and almost fell over.

'Where are you, Martha?' came Jonathan's voice, in just the same uneasy tones.

'I'm here. Where are you?'

'Here. Well, I was sitting on your bed and now I'm –ow!'

There was a crash and a chair not far from Martha's bed fell over. The only little difficulty they had both forgotten struck them at the same moment. They were both invisible, as they had wished. And of course they were both invisible to each other as well.

'Here I am!' came Jonathan's voice at Martha's side.

'Yes, you put your finger in my eye – do be careful,' she scolded.

'Martha!' Her mother's voice called up the stairs. 'I'm going now – do you want a lift or are you going to walk?'

'I can't answer,' whispered Martha. 'She'll come up and see I'm not here. If I walk she likes to get me out of the house and lock up after me. Oh, why didn't I think of this?'

'Write her a note as if you'd already left,' cried the resourceful Jonathan. 'Put it on your bed.'

So that was what Martha did, though it wasn't entirely easy writing with an invisible hand. She and Jonathan stood silently by the window listening to the door banging as other members of the family left, and then the stairs creaking as Mrs Grant came running up. She came into the room, read the note and ran downstairs again, to their great relief.

'They've all gone,' said Martha, after a moment. 'We'd better go out of the back door.'

The Grant family's morning routine was a rather complicated one, she realized, as she and Jonathan walked cautiously round the house to the front. First her father went off in his car to his school on the far side of the town where he was Head of the English Department. Then Anna and the boys raced off to catch the coach along with the other village children who went to the various secondary schools in town. Anna and the boys went to the same school, a comprehensive, but it was not the school where their father taught. That would have been a quite impossible situation, as everybody was agreed. Mrs Grant taught French in a girls' convent school set in its own grounds not far from the village, so she drove off in her car a little after everybody else. And Martha, usually with Jonathan, walked to the village school, some ten minutes away. She had plenty of time for the walk, usually arriving at school rather early. Sometimes this earliness was boring but today she looked forward to it eagerly.

A little more used to their invisibility now, they walked hand in hand, so that each knew where the other was, along the road towards the village green. On reaching the green they saw that the older school children's coach must be late, for there was a great collection, about thirty of them, standing with their cases and bags, chatting and laughing together. It only occasionally happened that Martha and Jonathan saw this group all together as they had usually already left by the time the primary school children were on their way.

So it was with some interest that Martha watched Anna, in all her sixth form dignity, looking very bored and grown-up talking to a little group of girls her own age, rather apart from the others. As the age range was from eleven to eighteen, the secondary school lot came in all shapes and sizes, of course: some of them being not much bigger than Jonathan and Martha.

There was Mark with a group of twelve-year-old boys standing a little uneasily as they watched some bigger boys, fourteen-year-olds, scuffling about and banging each other with their brief cases. There was Paul somewhere in the middle of the scuffling – and Martha as she passed quite close to him was suddenly struck by the look of misery in his eyes.

She saw the big, burly figure of fifteen-year-old Kevin Carter and he had the much smaller Paul by the back of the neck and was hitting him. There was a good deal of laughing and shouting from the other boys, and Martha could see that Paul was trying to fight back, but not getting much chance.

'He's a great bully and yob, that Kevin,' breathed Jonathan in Martha's ear. 'He beat up somebody at school last week and knocked out two of his teeth; his brother was telling us all about it.'

'I think Paul's friends ought to help him more,' exclaimed Martha indignantly. They were just standing, laughing, even if it was rather uneasy laughter.

'How can they?' asked Jonathan. 'You don't want to get on the wrong side of Kev Carter.'

'I believe Paul's been on the wrong side of him all this term, now I come to think of it,' exclaimed Martha, realizing that a lot of little things she had barely noticed in Paul's behaviour this term added up to just that: he was being bullied.

He had taken to looking very white and miserable some- times at breakfast and bit your head off if you asked him if he was feeling all right. He didn't seem to have any friends now. He was more and more on his own. Mark was all right, always had been; good at games, energetic, outgoing and noisy. Paul was quieter, liked reading, was conscientious over homework and hadn't grown much lately. It was only the other day that Martha noticed that Mark had nearly caught him up in size; only a year or so previously Paul had been much the taller of the two.

'Oo – look at 'is nice 'ittle pencil case then,' Kevin cried, snatching the pencil case from Paul's bulging school bag.

'Hi, give that back, it's new,' cried Paul, indignantly reaching after it.

But Kevin Carter held it out of his reach, laughing at his vain efforts to get at it and then turned to climb on the coach which had just drawn up. All the other boys and girls, on seeing the coach, came pushing and shoving up to climb aboard and Paul was pushed aside. Martha saw Kevin and two of his friends go right to the back where they sat down, looking triumphantly at Paul, who was forced to sit halfway down the coach with the others of his particular year.

Martha and Jonathan could see how impossible it was for Paul to go and reclaim his pencil case. Now the coach was filling up and Anna and her friends condescended to notice it and get on, where they sat at the front near the driver, quite unaware of what was going on behind them.

'That pencil case.' Martha's eyes filled with sympathetic tears for Paul. 'He spent a lot of money on it only last week because he said his last one was nicked. And he had to get new geometry instruments and everything. He cares about his things. It isn't as if it was Mark, who always loses everything and laughs. Oh, poor Paul.'

She and Paul hadn't spoken much to one another lately. But it was Paul who had taught her how to row on their summer holidays last year. And it was Paul who helped her with her sums and who had read most to her when she was little and couldn't read well for herself. Even if the books he read were more suitable for a nine-year-old boy than a five-year-old girl, Martha had appreciated the thought and taken quite an interest in the Jennings stories and in endless facts about cars and aeroplanes. Paul could be very thoughtful and kind, and he was her brother and she couldn't bear to see Kevin getting the better of him. Normally Martha would have been very frightened of Kevin but suddenly she realized her advantage.

'Come on,' she urged Jonathan. 'We must get on that coach. I'm going to get that pencil case back.'

'But, Martha – ' he objected.

She had dropped his hand and vanished somewhere into the depths of the coach. Jonathan climbed the steps and stood near the entrance – of course he couldn't see her. Most of the boys and girls were settling down in their seats now: there were some empty places, but the coach would stop again for another intake nearer the town.

Jonathan had little fear of anybody knocking into him at the moment but he wished Martha would hurry up doing whatever she was doing. The coach would go; couldn't she see? And indeed, as he was realizing this very thing the doors folded inwards, the driver settled in his seat, the engine started up, and suddenly they were off.

They were shut in, trapped in the school coach, bound for town which was miles away from their village and the homely little school where they had planned to have such fun!

Martha saw and felt the coach move but the full anguish of it did not strike her as it had struck Jonathan; she was much too occupied in working out how to snatch Paul's pencil case for him. She crouched down in the aisle just before and to the right of Kevin who fortunately was sitting on an outside seat. He had the pencil case on his lap and was taking out its contents and holding them up for the amusement of his friends.

'Like this pair o' compasses, Dale? I've already got one of them.'

As the pair of compasses was held up and the other boy was reaching out for it, Martha made a wild snatch and wrenched it out of Kevin's hand, gouging his wrist slightly with it as she did so. Almost at the same time, with her other had she seized the pencil case from Kevin's knee.

"'Ere, what?" he bellowed, staring about him and obviously expecting to find Paul somewhere near. But there was nobody to be seen. The stupefied expression of disbelief on his face was very funny to see, had Martha had time to linger. But she realized that though she was holding the two objects in her invisible hands they remained perfectly visible and as if supported in the air. Her one wish was to get them to Paul as quickly as possible and she raced down the coach with them and threw them on the startled Paul's knees, leaving pandemonium behind her.

Not only Kevin and his friend Dale but several other boys and girls had seen the incredible sight of a pencil case and a pair of compasses moving on their own down the coach.

'What? Did you see? How?' came from several sides, while Paul clutched the pencil case and with trembling hands tried to put the pair of compasses into it.

'How did that happen?' Several people were out of their seats now, moving about excitedly. One girl held up a crayon which had fallen out of the moving pencil case on to her knee. 'How did that get here?' she kept on asking.

Martha was pushed and kicked, and retreated to stand beside Jonathan at the top of the bus. The driver, hearing the noise and excitement, pulled his coach into the side of the road and turned round in his seat.

'Here you lot, belt up!' he shouted. 'Go and sit down or I don't take you.'

'It's a poltergeist!' shouted somebody jokingly. 'Watch out, there's a poltergeist loose in this coach!'

'What's a poltergeist?' whispered Jonathan to Martha as the coach lumbered into motion again.

'A kind of ghost that throws things about – I think,' replied Martha uncertainly.

Very soon the coach stopped again for its second intake, and to avoid being kicked and punched, Martha and Jonathan were forced right down to the back of the coach which was already full, to stand near Kevin and his friends. Martha was pleased to notice that Kevin looked rather white and thoughtful and occasionally nursed his wounded wrist.

When the coach drew up at the school Martha and Jonathan managed to duck down into a seat which had been vacated rather early by its occupant who was eager to get out of the coach quickly, but it was a near thing. Both of them were shaking and trembling by the time they managed to sneak off the coach after everybody else. It had not been a pleasant experience, shut in with so many heedless, excited people who couldn't see them.

'What shall we do now?' They stood in the playground watching all the boys and girls stream into the school.

'We'd better wait until they've all gone – ' Martha was just beginning when another coach drew up bringing the intake from another village, and a fresh crowd surged towards them. She and Jonathan, who had been touching each other but not holding hands firmly, were swept apart; Martha having received a blow in her back stumbled a few paces, recovered herself and to save herself was forced to run ahead of a close knit group of people, had no time to dodge another group coming from a different direction and willy-nilly was swept through the open doors of the school into a corridor. It was impossible to remain there in safety, so she moved again into what looked like a dining hall where she retreated to a corner, shaken, bemused and with no idea of Jonathan's whereabouts or how she could possibly meet up with him. One thing was certain, she could not possibly move about until the school had settled down and all the moving throng of boys and girls gone to their respective classrooms.

Bells rang, there was a distant hubbub of feet and voices and then a blessed stillness and silence descended on the school. Martha emerged from her corner and, feeling strangely self-conscious despite her invisibility, crept over the polished floors, her footsteps frighteningly loud, towards the school doors. But she was headed off by a couple of men striding rapidly towards her, holding piles of books and talking hard.

'The problem with 5E as I see it,' one was saying, 'is the whole problem of the structure of their day . . .' They turned abruptly down another corridor, driving Martha before them.

She had to dodge into the open door of the library to escape. The library was deserted so she moved further into it and then was horrified to see the enquiring face of the librarian, a little woman in horn-rimmed glasses, peering round one of the bookcases towards her in evident puzzlement, having obviously been alerted by the sound of Martha's footsteps.

In something resembling panic Martha ran off, deeper into the school, passing notice boards, art displays, lecture theatres, all deserted. Now she could hear some rather ragged singing and a piano and through an interior glass window glimpsed the whole school at Assembly. She didn't want to get caught up with them as they all came out, so began to retrace her steps past a door marked "Boys".

It opened suddenly as she passed it and a breath of cigarette smoke drifted out, followed by Kevin Carter and his friend Dale. They began, rather furtively, to move quietly down the corridor ahead of Martha. Martha, a little bolder now, could not resist the temptation. She resolved to strike a final blow for Paul, and putting her hands to her mouth to alter the sound, she boomed after them as loudly as she could:

'Kevin Carter! Beware!'

He and Dale spun round to gaze in fright and disbelief down the empty corridor.

'Beware!' boomed Martha again, beginning to enjoy herself. 'This is the poltergeist speaking!'

'Wha – what?' Kevin and Dale looked round them blankly, their mouths open.

'Leave boys smaller than yourselves alone,' trumpeted Martha. She decided not to mention Paul by name. 'Fight your own size if you *must* fight! Beware or I shall haunt you. Beware!'

She flitted past them, tweaking Kevin's jacket and tugging at his tie as she did so. She was beginning to feel almost sorry for him, he looked so frightened and amazed. She heard him say to Dale, ''Ere, let's get out,' and was amused to see both boys race down the corridor in panic and disappear.

That ought to fix them, thought Martha, tip-toeing after them. But she did wish she could meet up with Jonathan.

She retraced her steps to a meeting place of various corridors, where there was the art display and notice boards and a few seats and was delighted to see a rather curious sight. A chair moved on its own across the floor, to stand in the middle of the open space. As she watched, a vase of flowers came to join it and then a pile of books moving neatly through the air together.

'Jonathan!' cried Martha in relief.

'I'm getting ready to be a poltergeist,' came Jonathan's voice. 'When people start coming down the corridor I shall throw some books, and give them something to wonder about.'

'I was a poltergeist too,' said Martha proudly. 'I didn't half fix that Kevin Carter. I – '

'They're coming!' whispered Jonathan.

A file of smaller ones, first years, accompanied by a mistress walking along beside them, saying: 'Quietly, quietly, don't run – *single* file please,' approached them from a long corridor.

Jonathan hastily stood on the chair, holding the vase of flowers in one hand.

'Ow!' shrieked a girl. 'Look!'

The vase of flowers, apparently suspended high in mid-air slowly tipped itself up, water and flowers spraying out of it.

Then for good measure Jonathan climbed on the chair again with a pile of books and began throwing them one by one in different directions.

There was a pandemonium of shrieks and shouts. Other people, alerted by the hubbub, began to appear from doors and other corridors calling, 'What's happening!' or 'Quiet, *please*! Have you all gone mad?'

'Quick!' Martha felt her wrist seized. 'Let's get out while we can!'

Holding tightly to one another they moved as quickly as they could out of the school.

'That was good,' said Jonathan with satisfaction when they were safely out in the car park in the front of the school.

'Yes, it was,' Martha agreed. 'That Kevin Carter is a big coward, too. I wonder where he ran off to? And Jonathan, I wonder how we are going to get back to *our* school?'

* * *

Two hours later a weary and still invisible Jonathan and Martha plodded up the winding country lane leading to their village school. They had found out how to get back: by walking. They had discussed stealing a ride on a bus which would have taken them some of the way, but decided against it, the buses were too full, and besides they were uncertain which one to take. It would have been dreadful to have been swept off in the wrong direction – and invisible people can't ask questions. Not if they want sane answers.

So walking it had been, and walking a long distance on a warm day is just as tiring when one is invisible as when one is visible.

When they finally reached their school the bell was ringing and it was dinner time. Martha and Jonathan were able to tag on to the end of a queue of children waiting to be served at the dining hatches. But they were still invisible.

'We said we wanted to be visible by dinner time,' whispered Jonathan fiercely to Martha. 'And we're not. It isn't fair! I want my dinner.'

'Jonathan, I've just thought of something awful,' she exclaimed. 'Do you think Mrs Tom knows what time we have dinner here? It's much earlier than home, isn't it? At home we have it about one o'clock but at school it's twelve-fifteen, isn't it? Do you think we're going to stay invisible for another three-quarters of an hour?'

'Oh *no*!' groaned Jonathan.

But that was precisely what happened. Too tired and dispirited to cause any more 'poltergeist' happenings, they eventually managed to get into the kitchens behind the backs of the cooks who were busy serving, and stole some rolls and salad, and had a long drink at the tap of the big sink. Even then one of the cooks turned round in surprise at hearing the tap running, and came across to turn it off, and Jonathan only just got out of her way in time.

It was a blessed relief when finally, as they followed their friends out into the playground, they suddenly found themselves visible again.

'Hullo,' said her friend Mandy casually to Martha. 'Where

did *you* come from? Been skiving? You missed a horrible Arithmetic test, you beast.'

When Anna, Paul and Mark came back from school that afternoon they were full of stories about the poltergeist, or whatever it had been, on the coach to school and at school.

'Kev Carter wasn't there at dinner time, or on the coach coming back,' Paul kept on saying, his eyes shining. 'They said he didn't feel well and had gone home. And I don't know *how* I got my pencil case back, but here it is! It's the most extraordinary thing that's ever happened to me.'

'One B saw this vase emptied and the books moving about,' cried Mark. 'I wish I had!'

'One B are potty if you ask me,' sniffed Anna. '*I* didn't see anything.'

'But, Anna, I heard Miss Lawrence talking to Mr Dudley. She saw it happen too,' argued Mark. 'She said she couldn't believe her eyes, but there was the mess on the floor to prove it.'

'Poltergeist happenings *can* occur in schools sometimes, I believe,' said Anna, beginning to be convinced despite herself. 'I was reading a book about them. But they have to be set off by somebody in particular – some disturbed child or adolescent.'

Martha and Jonathan, who was having tea with them, kicked each other under the table and grinned.

'Oh, as for disturbed adolescents,' cried Paul cheerfully, 'there are plenty enough of them at our school. It could be anybody. You know – I'm not going to let that Kev Carter bug me again. Even if he does try it on – I'm not really scared of him now. In fact I'm sorry for him, really,' he finished loftily. 'It must be awful to have a brain the size of a pin's head.'

'If Kevin bothers you, just tell me,' cried Anna. 'I know his older brother. In fact he quite fancies me – not that he's got much chance. But a word from me – and he'll keep that slob of a Kevin in order.'

'Probably won't be necessary.' Paul began to whistle. He

was a changed boy; as if a great load had been lifted from his shoulders.

'Is Jonathan staying on to supper?' asked Anna. 'Mummy and Daddy are going out and I'm doing lots of sausages. I don't mind doing one or two more for him.'

It turned out to be a lively evening; one of the best Martha had ever had. Jonathan stayed on and apart from him it was just the four of them; no Steve, no friend of Mark's. Everything went right, everybody seemed gay and friendly and nobody was in a bad mood. Oh, if only life could be like that more often! Anna made an elaborate pudding to go after the sausages and she let Martha help her and didn't shout at her or have an attack of cook's temperament because the pudding wasn't turning out right – and Martha didn't spill anything and was allowed to lick out the bowl afterwards which was covered with an extremely rich chocolate goo.

During supper, which, assisted by Toby, they all had together in the kitchen (nobody snubbing or shouting at anybody else) it grew very dark, far darker than the time of evening warranted.

'There must be going to be a storm,' exclaimed Anna.

Outside the kitchen window the clouds hung, low and black. The green of the garden was intensely green in livid contrast; the very air seemed coloured a heavy, dark green. Then it was lit up by a great white flash.

'Count!' cried Martha excitedly and she and Jonathan counted. 'One, two, three,' and then there was a great rumble of thunder.

'Three miles. The storm is three miles away,' cried Martha.

'I hope it comes right overhead,' exclaimed Paul. Hardly had he spoken when there was another flash followed almost instantly by an ear-splitting loud clap of thunder. As if some tap in the sky had been suddenly turned full on it began to pelt with rain in a continuous dark downpour.

'Windows!' shouted Anna, leaping from her seat at the table. 'We'd better shut all the windows!'

Martha rushed to her room to fasten her window and

found the rain indeed coming in and Mrs Tom, her umbrella up to protect herself, walking to and fro on the carpet just below.

'Very refreshing,' she remarked to Martha, 'but you can shut it now or our house will turn into Noah's Ark, and float away.'

'How did the invisibility go?' called Mr Tom, who was sitting just inside his house.

'Well – odd. It was odd. Not what I'd thought it would be like. But we did play a few tricks and we didn't half show that Kevin Carter. He was bullying Paul. Paul is so happy now. And we're all having such fun!'

Martha gave Mr Tom a beaming smile. She was still so pleased for Paul. She could hear him and Mark and Jonathan chasing each other over the house and giggling hysterically. Toby was barking and altogether there was a lovely shindy.

'The boys and girls on the school coach thought we were poltergeists,' Martha told the Toms.

'I daresay they did.' Mrs Tom shook out the rain from her umbrella and folded it.

'Mrs Tom, these poltergeists, I've been wondering. Are they all children like us who've been turned invisible and are playing tricks on people?'

Mrs Tom looked rather amused.

'The world is a good deal more complicated than that,' she said. 'Though from time to time it must have happened through a wish. But there are very, very few people about now who are able to grant wishes. And there have been lots of poltergeists plaguing people throughout the centuries.'

'I wish – no, I don't – I mean I would like you to tell me more about all sorts of things,' continued Martha thoughtfully. 'We've only three wishes left and I want to make them really good ones. I don't want to say goodbye to you. I suppose I will have to say goodbye to you when my wishes are over?'

'I expect you will,' said Mrs Tom shortly.

'Can't you give us any idea about a really good wish to make?' persisted Martha. 'The ones we make on our own don't always seem to turn out as we think they will.'

100

Mr Tom climbed out of his house and went to stand near his wife.

'No, I'm afraid we can't,' he said regretfully.

'Not allowed.' Mrs Tom bit her lips as if to keep something in.

Something in the intensity with which they were looking up at her struck Martha. They moved near together and Mr Tom put his hand lightly about his wife's shoulder, and for once she didn't knock it away.

A far-away, long-drawn-out rumble sounded. The thunder was passing over, moving on. The rain had slackened, though it still fell steadily. It was much colder.

'Martha!' came Anna's voice. 'Martha, come down. We've got a fire going and we're roasting marshmallows. Don't you want any?'

'Oh, gorgeous!' cried Martha in delight.

A fire in summer, a thunderstorm, marshmallows, everybody together and in a zany, excited mood, no parents – what magic could be better than this?

Difficult things like wishes could be postponed, and so, hastily saying goodnight to the Toms, she ran downstairs to the others who were already holding melting marshmallows to the flames. The edge of the marshmallow nearest the fire slowly turned brown, then it moved and bubbled and then the blackening skin slid off and the runny part underneath it tried to fall to the hearth and Martha caught it just in time and popped the whole delicious mess into her mouth, trying not to burn her tongue.

'I wonder if we'll have any more poltergeist happenings at school,' said Paul dreamily, licking his fork.

'I don't think you will,' Martha told him.

'How do you know?' Anna asked her with an air of authority and knowledge. 'Once these phenomena start they can go on for weeks.'

Martha said nothing, but she caught Jonathan's eye and they winked at one another. The storm was nearly over now.

'Perhaps it was just the electricity in the air, before the

storm, I mean,' suggested Mark. 'Electricity does odd things, doesn't it?'

And they left it at that, rather sleepy and pleasantly warm and full and happy as they all were, listening to the sizzling of the fire and the rain falling.

9

Martha had been thinking very deeply. It had quite hurt her head. And the results of her thoughts were as follows. Apart from the flying wish, which had been pure enjoyment, in a sense the most successful things about their wishes had been indirect, like buying her father's picture, and rescuing Paul from Kevin Carter. If these good things had resulted from their more selfish wishes, what goodness might not result from a truly *un*selfish wish, made directly for others, for her family? Kind, noble and giving: that was to be her aim in future.

So what was she going to wish for her family? While she was thinking, Martha decided to brighten everybody's lives by introducing a little gracious living into the scene; she would make a truly beautiful flower arrangement for the supper table. Humming a jaunty hymn tune to herself, she went out into the garden . . .

'Yes, Martha, those tulips do look lovely with the wild flowers you've collected, I quite agree, but I rather wish you hadn't taken just those very ones by the front gate,' said her mother distractedly, moving between oven, larder and kitchen table. 'And could you get water from the downstairs lav, darling, and *not* the kitchen sink. You're in my way dreadfully there.'

'Oh, I'm always shouted at and wrong!' cried Martha, feeling very unappreciated. Nobody else thought of flowers, or could arrange them like herself – if only the wretched tulips wouldn't keep on falling out and bringing everything else with them.

'Oh, Martha, just look at the mess!'

'All right, all right, all *right*. I was just going to mop it up. You never tell Anna off like you tell me off.'

'Well, Anna doesn't get under my feet just as I'm dishing up. It's a lovely collection of flowers, darling – if you'd just take it right out of my way.'

'You never tell the boys off, either,' grumbled Martha. Waves of emotion swept over her; life was always like this, in her family. Unloved, her efforts unthanked, she was the poor Cinderella, the butt of them all.

'The boys don't arrange flowers just before supper either, and I told you it's a pretty collection, Martha. Now do be reasonable,' and her mother's voice began to rise as she hastily rushed to take a saucepan off the boil.

Reasonable was not what Martha wanted to be, just then. She was in a bad mood because a good idea was going all wrong, and she wanted to find a scapegoat, somebody to blame. The others were coming into the kitchen now. Paul began to lay the table, it being his turn, Anna filled herself a glass of water from the sink and Mark began to wander in and out of the back door and through the kitchen with his gerbil's cage, having chosen just that minute to clean it out. Meanwhile the telephone rang and everybody jumped; Martha could hear them all thinking 'Is it for me?' She knew it wouldn't be for *her*: nobody ever rang *her* up, at least hardly anybody.

But it was for her father, they heard him talking, loudly and jovially from the hall, the voice he put on for the deputy head at his school who was an immense talker and a great friend of his.

'Oh, my goodness, that's Daddy out for half an hour at least,' cried Martha's mother. 'Just as I had supper ready and wanted to dish up.'

'Come on,' urged Paul and Anna together. 'We're hungry.'

'What are we having?' called Mark from the open back door. Sawdust blew back into the kitchen as he spoke.

'Mince, and for goodness sake, Mark, put that cage away and shut the door. Martha, *please* put those flowers down and stop fiddling with them.'

'Ugh, not mince again,' said Paul in disgust. 'Mince with spuds or mince with worms?'

'I wish you wouldn't call spaghetti "worms",' cried Anna, wincing away from Paul in refined horror. 'You are disgusting. And you, too, Martha, can't you see you've slopped water on the table?'

'Mop it up then,' cried Martha.

'Not my turn to do the table today. Mop it up yourself. Or Paul can.'

'I don't see why I should mop up Martha's mess. Here, call that a flower arrangement? It's pathetic. You've got a forget-me-not completely upside down.'

'Oh – I wish you . . .' Martha was just beginning vehemently when the word 'wish' suddenly caught her attention before she could finish the sentence, which was going to be 'I wish you would shut up'. Although it was very unlikely that Mr and Mrs Tom would hear her so far away, supposing they had very acute ears and granted her wish? Would Paul shut up? Would they interpret it literally and keep him silent all evening, or kind of folded in on himself – that kind of shut up? Martha surprised herself by giving a loud snort of laughter. Suddenly everything seemed much better. She could even take the pressures of family life in her stride. So she got a cloth and mopped the table and put the forget-me-not the right way up, all in a happy haze, and presently supper was dished up and they all ate peacefully; Mr Grant arriving about halfway through and catching them up with great rapidity.

'The rate you shovel food in, Daddy, is quite disgusting,' said Anna faintly, closing her eyes.

'You leave Daddy alone,' cried Martha, as always her father's champion.

Apart from that, not much was said, and as Martha ate her way through her mince and potatoes she resolved to tell Jonathan her latest thoughts about wishes at the earliest opportunity. The next day was Saturday, so they should have plenty of free time.

Surprisingly enough, Jonathan, next day, was not so keen on the idea of brightening the lives of Martha's family as she would have wished.

'Well, what do you want for them anyway?' he said at last, grudgingly.

'Oh, I don't know,' exclaimed Martha impatiently. 'There must be something. If I can just think what.'

There was silence for a few seconds. Her mind was a complete blank. What on earth could her family, as such, desire?

'Come on, what?' said Jonathan again.

'Oh, like a good holiday for us all, and Anna wanting to come too,' cried Martha in desperation.

'That's awfully boring,' said Jonathan. 'And how do I come into that? What about me and my family?'

'Oh, OK, OK,' said Martha a little crossly. 'But I still think we ought to ask for something really worthwhile – like to be perfectly happy, or something.'

'That wouldn't work,' said Jonathan with certainty. 'The Toms couldn't keep it up. And then one would have to go back to being unhappy again – well, not unhappy, I suppose, but normal. And the normalness would seem worse then. No – I think you're being rather boring with your ideas. Let's do something really exciting for a change. I mean something really adventurous, like visiting somewhere strange. America, perhaps.'

'America isn't that strange,' said Martha a little huffily. 'Anyway, I'd rather go to Africa. See all the zebras and things in their natural places. And the darling gorillas.'

'I know!' Jonathan suddenly shouted. 'Space travel! Why didn't I think of it before? I don't expect I'd ever get chosen as an astronaut in the normal way. We could visit another planet.'

'I'm not sure about that,' said Martha dubiously. 'We'd need space suits and things. And it would be an awful long way to go. I think I'd rather just fly again than do that.'

'But don't you see, we can just wish anything. You're thinking in a straight line, like we did with the money wish.

Flying could be a part of the space wish, probably. It's all how we say it. It's up to the Toms.'

'I don't know if they could manage a big wish like a space wish,' said Martha hesitantly.

'How do you know? Come on, let's go and talk to them.'

So Martha let herself be persuaded, and they went up into her room where Martha knew she would find Mr and Mrs Tom quite lively and prepared for more effort.

On entering they found both the Toms out walking in the middle of the carpet, to and fro. They did not walk together, but their paths crossed from time to time.

'Good afternoon,' cried Mr Tom to them with his usual courtesy. 'Just taking a little constitutional, as you see. Fine day, isn't it?'

'They'll be wanting another wish,' said Mrs Tom, without pausing in her marching to and fro. She was using her umbrella as a walking stick.

'Yes, please,' said Jonathan eagerly, and then before Martha could say anything he was asking, 'Can you give us a space wish? We want to travel in space.'

'Where do you want to go?' tossed Mrs Tom over her shoulder, as she turned sharply on one heel and set off on a course between Martha's bedside chair and the old record player she had inherited from Anna.

'You mean we can?' cried Jonathan. 'Can we fly to – let me think – I suppose Tau Ceti and Epsilon Epidaurus are rather far away? I read somewhere that they may be the nearest planets to ours which have life on them.'

'So you read wrong.' Mrs Tom shrugged her shoulders.

'You mean we'd have to go further off? But then we'd get into a muddle with light years, wouldn't we? We don't want to be old people by the time we return!'

'I'm not going if it's going to be like that!' flashed Martha quickly. 'Really, Jonathan, I haven't said you could wish that wish anyway.'

'Make your minds up,' said Mrs Tom making straight for them as they sat together on the floor. At the last moment she turned, and was off at a tangent on a course that took her somewhere right under Martha's bed, where she was lost from view.

'She's a great one for exercise,' said Mr Tom coming to a halt beside Jonathan. 'Now I'm a moderate sort of fellow as you know, and so I'm quite glad of a little rest. There's no sort of difficulty about the wish you suggest. We can find life within our own solar system you know, no need to look outside it. Where do you want to go? The moon's a bit of a risk, I suppose, in that there might not be anybody on it right now. It doesn't have its own life, but attracts a good deal of callers from time to time who use it as a base. There *is* life on Venus of a sort, but it's like a great cooking pot there; everything bubbling away and nothing cooked yet and ready to grow. To be safe I should think we'd better go to Mars. You earth people may think there is no life there, but you're quite wrong. No problem. You want to fly there you say? I'll have to consult my wife over that one – Mrs T! Er – just come over here a moment, my dear. Do you have any objection to Mars this afternoon? They want to fly if possible.'

He said it as matter of factly as if it were as simple as catching a train to Surbiton.

'It's your wish this time,' she reminded him, suddenly emerging from under the bed into a beam of sunlight. 'I suppose I'd better come along though, to keep an eye on things. It's still *extremely dirty* under your bed, Martha. I think I've spoken to you before about telling your maidservant off.'

' – Er, that was my mother,' said Martha, but Mrs Tom wasn't listening. She had out her little notebook and pencil.

'To Mars then, the flying route,' she said as she wrote. 'Mr Tom in charge. The weather's too fine for me to concentrate well, it hurts my eyes. Come along then, Jonathan, the wish must be spoken properly, out loud, before we can get under way.'

And so Jonathan, his face alight with anticipation, spoke the wish: 'We wish to fly to Mars, please.'

There was a swirling, giddy sensation and Martha had a quick glimpse of both Mr and Mrs Tom standing rigidly together, their eyes shut, a look of supreme concentration on their faces, and then she found herself rising. She put out her hands, thinking she was going to touch the ceiling – had she floated out of the window somehow? If she had, a mist must have come up for although there was a diffused light glowing around her, the sun was obscured, everything was obscured except herself and Jonathan – and Mr and Mrs Tom. But there was something different about them – it took her a second or so to realize what it was.

Why, they were growing! Either that, or she was shrinking. Mr Tom was now distinctly taller than she, much taller, nearer her own father in size, a man of middle height. His wife, though a good deal smaller than he, was now about five feet or so; a perfectly possible size for a small but fully grown woman to be.

Together the four of them were floating briskly upwards surrounded by white mist.

'You're drifting off course – hold my umbrella,' said Mrs Tom to Martha. 'Tom, catch hold of that boy, keep him with you.'

'Oh – come on, Jonathan, my lad – here's my hand. Exhilarating isn't it?' called Tom enthusiastically. 'I always feel on these occasions like making up poetry – it's the release from the body that does it.'

'Why have you grown? Is that your normal size?' asked Jonathan, eyeing him.

'Yes, indeed. I'm out of that puny little enchanted bit of nonsense, thank goodness. Now you see me in my aetherial form which approximates closely to my true earthly form and is much more comfortable for travelling. It's the same for you, you know.'

'Where are we?' asked Martha, not quite understanding Mr Tom's words but letting them pass. 'We don't seem to be anywhere exactly. I'm not sure I like it very much.'

'You wanted to fly, didn't you?' snapped Mrs Tom. 'This is the only way – through the Astral Projection, into another sphere altogether. It has it's disadvantages – but this is Mr Tom's affair. I don't doubt he knows what he's doing – if he concentrates. Look at the silly old fool now – trying to sing. Better stuff your ears with something – '

Martha thought Mrs Tom was being rather rude for Mr Tom had a pleasant, tuneful baritone: 'I dreamt that I dwe – helt – in marble halls,' he carolled. 'And you lo- huved me still the sa-hame.'

They floated onwards; at least it was difficult to have much sensation of movement; the mist could just as well have been swirling backwards past them.

'I can see other people,' said Martha, doubtfully, peering through the mist. She was dimly aware of other forms in the mist, wandering in different directions. Then a crowd of little shapes seemed to blow towards them. Suddenly they were among a throng of them: it was difficult to tell if they were animal or human, for they were not solid and you could see through them: smallish creatures with half human faces and staring greenish eyes. They floated about Martha and Jonathan, trying to catch on to them, plucking at their clothes and gently pulling their hair.

'Nasty creatures! Get away!' cried Mrs Tom, vigorously slashing at them with her umbrella. The misty creatures had very little power, and were soon dislodged, but they were distinctly unpleasant, even frightening. One could just feel them on one, like spiders.

'I don't like them!' wailed Martha, after Mrs Tom had dislodged a softly clinging shape from her back: 'What are they?'

'Creatures who don't have bodies and want them,' said Mrs Tom shortly. 'Get off, you! They can't hurt, but they will cluster round anything with life in it. Sometimes they get down to earth and – ugh – there's one in my umbrella. Tom! Tom! What are you about? Isn't there a better way in? Must we tangle with all these wretched little elementals?'

'Nearly there now,' cried Mr Tom, still leading them. 'We should be finding the way in any minute – ah – do you see the reddish tint? The rift is beginning . . .'

'Martha, Jonathan, hold my umbrella and shut your eyes,' commanded Mrs Tom. 'If you look now you'll only get giddy.'

Martha and Jonathan did as they were bid; Martha's eyes flickering open once to see an incredible sideways view of mountains and rock, all at an angle, as if they or she were sideways on, closed her eyes again, felt a great wind, then a slight sensation of dropping – and opened her eyes to find herself standing on a red, sandy desert with rocks and boulders poking through great orange-coloured dunes of sandy earth. The sky was pinkish. The sun was setting on the horizon, and on the other side of the pale sky stars were already appearing. She saw a small white disc which at first she took to be the moon but it was smaller. Then she realized that on Mars one couldn't see the Earth Moon – perhaps this was Mars's own moon. She didn't know if Mars had a moon or not. She pointed it out to Jonathan.

'Mars has two moons,' he said authoritatively. 'They are called Phoebos and Demos. I don't know which that is, actually. Honestly, Martha, don't you know *anything* about astronomy?'

'I don't know much about astronomy perhaps but I do know a lot more than you do about all sorts of other things!' retorted Martha with heat. To tell the truth, she was a little disappointed in Mars. The colours were beautiful and there was certainly a strange unearthly feel about it – but when all was said and done it was just a desert, without any life at all as far as she could see, and she was rather shaken up by her journey and apprehensive; feeling a very, very long way from home.

'I wonder what that is?' said Jonathan, pointing.

'What?'

'Far away, not far from the horizon. A column of something. It's moving, I think.'

'Where? I can't see anything.'

'If we just climb up and over these rocks we might have a better view. Look, there. Don't you see it now?'

'Yes, I think I do. It's a tall – I think it's growing. And it's getting nearer.'

Martha and Jonathan continued to look out from the rocks on to which they had clambered. The ground fell away steeply below them on one side to a sandy gully; beyond, and still below them sand dunes stretched in undulating orange waves as far as they could see. The object they watched looked a little like a dark, tall rock, but it was rotating, moving at what was obviously a great speed, though it was still too far off to tell exactly what it was. There was no other sign of life in the desert, no plants, no animals, no birds. You could almost hear the stillness and silence, it was so strong.

Then Martha thought she could hear a noise; a kind of hissing, rushing noise. At the same time a gentle breeze lifted the hair from her forehead, let it drop again.

'It's growing taller – and fatter,' said Jonathan.

Neither Martha nor Jonathan realized that they were now some little distance from Mr and Mrs Tom. He had wandered off on a course of his own, his lips moving as if he were murmuring poetry to himself, while she had set out her open umbrella on the sand as a sunshade and was sitting beneath it, hugging her knees and looking as if she were disassociating herself from the entire expedition.

'It's much, much nearer,' said Jonathan suddenly.

As he spoke, the wind came again, blowing more strongly. At the same time Martha became aware of a high pitched whining, singing noise.

'Wee – ee, wee – ee.' Then she saw the sand on top of a ridge of dunes about a mile away begin to shiver and move, and blow up into the sky, as if it were being sucked.

'Martha – we're in its way – it's some kind of whirlwind or tornado,' said Jonathan suddenly.

'Let's go back to Mrs Tom,' cried Martha. So they began to scramble down from the rocks towards Mrs Tom, calling to her.

'Mrs Tom, Mrs Tom!'

They were near to her but not up to her and she was just beginning to turn and rise to her feet, when the noise intensified to an ear-splitting howling and keening: 'Weee – ee.' At the same time the sand and stones about their feet began to move and the wind hit them in a great blast. They clutched wildly for each other, but the wind was like a mad thing now: buffeting all round them, it got beneath their feet, lifted them, knocked the breath out of them, deafened them, tossed them and played with them, higher and higher . . . In a medley of flying sand and stones, first Jonathan and Martha, holding hands and then forced asunder, then Mrs Tom, desperately clinging to her umbrella into which the wind pounced and blew inside out, sending Mrs Tom head over heels, and then Mr Tom about fifty yards away turning to meet it, were lifted and blown and tossed like thistledown in one of the great winds of Mars, which reach for a mile or more into the sky and sing their own wild songs, the note deepening and intensifying as the wind grows ever stronger. Long red streamers of sand blew out from the heart of the storm, which covered an area of several miles, and grew in terrifying velocity with every minute. There was nothing but flying, dark confusion and crazy, nerve-wracking sound: 'Woo – eee, woo – ee, woo – oo': the mad song of a Martian sandstorm, too strong by far for human ears . . .

10

'Martha, Martha, wake up! Can you see anything?'

Martha had a confused impression of Jonathan shaking her by the arm; dazed, she sat up and found herself lying on some smooth, cool surface: there was a dim, purplish light.

Beside her Mrs Tom was sitting up, brushing sand from her dress. Overhead, the sky was clear and pale violet in colour, a few stars were beginning to twinkle. There was the remnant of the wind, a gentle, steady hissing and blowing sound came from somewhere, but around them the air was calm and still.

'Where are we? Where did we get to?' asked Martha in a dazed way, rubbing her eyes.

'I do hate a nasty wind like that,' said Mrs Tom crossly, getting to her feet and opening and closing her umbrella several times. 'The sand's got right into the folds. I *do* think Mr Tom could have managed it better – imagine taking us into the path of a storm. Even though we're out of our bodies and can't be badly hurt, we can certainly suffer a very unpleasant shock to the nervous system. Tom! Tom! Where are you?'

They looked about for him, but he was nowhere to be seen. The light was dim, and the view obstructed on either side by gently rising rocks. They seemed to be at the bottom of a long gully, or the dry bed of a river valley; but it was difficult to make it out exactly.

'Look under our feet,' exclaimed Martha suddenly.

She saw what the cool smooth surface was she had been lying on, it looked like marble, but varied in colour, as far as was possible to make out in the dim light.

'It's got a pattern!' Jonathan suddenly exclaimed. 'Zig-zags and circles – surely this has been *made*?'

114

'Mrs Tom, Mrs Tom,' Martha appealed to her. 'Look, this surely has been made, it can't be natural.'

'What's that? A pattern?' Mrs Tom's umbrella tip traced it out for a moment.

'So it is a pattern,' she said with unconcern. 'I wonder what that silly old fool is up to – he's no right to leave us like this. Mr Tom! Mr Tom!'

'But doesn't that mean somebody's made it – that there's life around here?' said Jonathan urgently.

'What's that! Of course there's life; that's what you wanted, isn't it? We're on somebody's drive I expect. Where did you think we were?'

'I don't know,' said Martha humbly. 'What shall we do now?'

'It's your wish,' said Mrs Tom firmly, compressing her lips. 'You'd better go on to the front door, hadn't you? Whether you'll like whoever opens it, I *don't* know. But I can see it's my duty to superintend – where *is* that blasted man?'

They walked along the patterned marble roadway; for this was certainly what it was. The banks on either side grew steeper; then they turned a corner, where a silvery light glowed and they found they had come upon a house made of dark stone and built into a rock face, with pink marble pillars and wide shallow steps up into an entrance which was illuminated somehow with softly glowing, silvery light.

'Er, how do we go inside?' wondered Jonathan, pausing at the bottom of the steps.

'*I* don't know.' Martha also hung back, feeling shy. She didn't even like calling on strangers on earth and being on Mars didn't seem to make it any better. What should she say? Would whoever came speak some utterly incomprehensible language? Would he *speak* at all – or have some other means of communication?

'Aren't you going to ring the bell?' demanded Mrs Tom at her side. 'What bell?' Both Martha and Jonathan looked about near what was obviously the front door of the house: a great slab of marble engraven with silver lines into what seemed an intricate design. It was hard to tell if the silver lines were an integral part of the marble or a natural vein running through it. But the door had nothing to pull, press or push and there was no knocker.

'Tch, tch,' said Mrs Tom impatiently beside Martha, and pushing her aside she marched up to the centre of the door and pressed a silver disc which Martha had taken to be a part of the design.

There was a clashing noise, like a pair of cymbals being gently struck and then the door hummed on a low note and slowly swung open, still humming.

Inside was more silvery light which looked as if it came from a fountain which splashed high in a great black basin: it was difficult to tell if it splashed water which was illuminated in some fashion, or a kind of liquid light, but neither Martha nor Jonathan had time to take it in for more than a moment because striding over the marbled hall to meet them came a tall figure, his arms outstretched in welcome. It was a figure which would have been disconcerting because of its height and strangeness were it not for the fact that a little behind it, quite at his ease, stood the figure of Mr Tom puffing away at his little clay pipe.

'Ah, there you are, my dear,' he said to his wife. 'Whatever took you so long?'

'This is the very *greatest* pleasure,' cried the tall Martian, bowing first over Martha, then Jonathan, then finally greeting Mrs Tom, who gave him a stiff little bow in return. 'First one of the earth Elders, which is rare enough, and then another, but better still, bringing two Earth children with them, of the younger race. *How* glad I am I didn't venture out this afternoon. My sister – and she will be disappointed, quite madly disappointed – said she must get a breath of air – she's ever such a one for communing with Nature – and so as there was this storm on she would go out into the thick of it, so cleansing and purifying, she said – and the result is that the silly girl has gone and missed your arrival. What luck I felt more like curling up with a good book! When Tom here arrived I said to myself delightedly, "Well just look what the wind's blown in!" but until he told me there would be more of

116

you I didn't realize quite what a haul it was. Now come in, right in, don't stand there in the hall (haul – hall – joke, my dears, do you see?). Let's go somewhere more comfortable where we can relax and talk at leisure. Are you feeling tired after your journey? Did the wind bother you? Come right through, darlings, and let me feast my eyes on you.'

Martha and Jonathan would have liked to return the compliment and feast their eyes on their host, but for a few minutes anyway they both felt too taken aback and shy to do anything but follow him as he walked in long, rather mincing strides along the length of his extensive hall through pillars of different colours and size, fountains of light and elegant, smooth artefacts which might be statues, though of what it was difficult to tell. Some of them were not unlike an exhibition of modern sculpture which Martha had once reluctantly seen. Then they found themselves in a large room of soft, beautiful colouring and flickering rosy light and with a huge window at the far side. They must have penetrated through the rock face into which the house was built because here was a grand view of moonlit and starlit gardens; rocks and what looked like winding roads cut through them, pillars and columns which obviously formed a part of some geometric design too complicated for the human eye to grasp easily, and above them a great dark-purple sky lit by the silver stars and now by the two moons, both risen in different quarters of the sky, small by Earth-moon standards but very bright indeed.

'Sit yourselves down,' cried the Martian, 'and let me get you a drink.'

They found that one of the glowing colours behind them was shaped like a great sofa: it seemed to be made of some crystalline stone, but its centre was heaped into something which glimmered like tinfoil or sheet metal but which was soft and resilient to sink into. So Martha and Jonathan, still speechless, sank into it while Mr and Mrs Tom took another sofa at an angle to theirs. Meanwhile the Martian brought them drinks in tall silver goblets: drinks which sparkled and fizzed and had a faint greenish colour.

117

'Ah nice,' said Mr Tom, taking a long drink and smacking his lips. 'Long time since I tasted this.'

'Thank you.' Mrs Tom, sitting bolt upright, her umbrella propped beside her, accepted the drink daintily, and sipped it. 'It's all right,' she said to Martha and Jonathan. 'You can drink it. It's only Martian water. It'll make your hair curl.'

'*Only* Martian water,' said the tall Martian, looking a little hurt. 'Water is one of our most precious substances, as you should know. What else should I offer my guests?'

'I'm sorry,' said Mrs Tom, looking a little abashed. 'It's only my way of speaking. Water here is indeed precious: and it tastes good, children. You try it.'

So Martha and Jonathan tried it, and liked its sparkling refreshing taste, and it must have given some courage to Jonathan, for he suddenly said to the Martian, 'Thank you. My name is Jonathan. What's yours?'

'My *dear* fellow I do apologize, how most frightfully rude of me,' cried the Martian, springing to his feet from the chair he had just taken. 'I am Marakite, of course, and my sister is Krita – only she's not here – and you are, Jonathan, and you are –'

'Martha,' replied Martha, also beginning to feel a good deal bolder, indeed quite relaxed and even slightly giggly. Marakite seemed so pleasant and so very polite and flattering. He was a remarkable-looking person too – very handsome in a way. Indeed she could hardly take her eyes off him. He was very tall indeed, about six foot six, and very thin, and he was clothed in some glistening, metallic-looking substance which changed shape as he moved but generally settled into something resembling a shirt-blouse on top, and knee breeches beneath the waist. His legs as far as his knees were clad in high black boots. His face and hands and hair was all nearly human – and yet not quite. At first glance he looked like a man with a very thin face and very sharp features – but there was something else. His skin glowed white, more like a precious stone – perhaps an opal – than like skin. His nose was very sharp – almost with a knife edge. The long fingers with which he handed her the drink were incredibly long and tapered for human fingers. The nails at the end were polished half moons of silver. His eyes were black and with painted eyebrows above, and his hair was black and long, fastened behind his head with a silver knot and falling to his collar. Hair was what Martha would have called it, for want of a better name, and yet it was not quite hair.

Martha took another draught of refreshing Martian water and blinked and looked again. Now she was looking closely she could see nothing of Marakite which looked fleshly and earthly: skin, or any hint of warm blood pulsing beneath it, or hair. His clothing was soft metal: what was he? Was he formed of metal too – or of stone? Was he a creature of crystal and jewel? She felt all her ideas about flesh and stone and metal and vegetable substances beginning to alter: perhaps they were more interchangeable, more malleable than she had thought. Perhaps you could *work* metal like wool, knit it: perhaps flesh could be solid as stone. Perhaps stone could breathe and talk . . .

She took another sip of her drink to steady herself. There was a metallic timbre to Marakite's voice: or was it more like a musical instrument through which one blew to make the sound? There was no equivalent on earth to his voice; and yet it was also very akin to an earthly man's voice, a tenor rather than a baritone.

'How is it you speak English?' she managed to ask him.

'I think it would be a *tiny* bit complicated to explain – really it could be any Earth language you see; it's a little akin to thought transference. But in any case I've been a student of Earth for many years – nearly all of us are, primitive races are *the* in thing at the moment and English is one of your principal languages, isn't it? It's a long time since I was down there and then the visit was rather fleeting, because you people are beginning to notice our spaceships rather more than we like, so please do keep me up to date on what is happening. I want to know *all* about both of you, where you live, what you eat for dinner – all sorts of fascinating things like that.'

Marakite was so easy to talk to, so flatteringly interested in what Martha and Jonathan had to say that they found

119

themselves telling him everything – about Martha and her brothers and sister and how frustrating it was always being the youngest, about Jonathan's being an only child and how boring that could be, and about the neighbourhood they lived in, their school, and holidays they had had. While thinking how to begin to tell Marakite about the sale and the weather house and how she felt she must own it, Martha glanced at Mr and Mrs Tom for the first time for many minutes to find them both slumped back in their sofa fast asleep. The faintest frisson of unease went over her to see them thus: and also a feeling of embarrassment for them, it didn't seem very polite. Beside the elegant Martian, they looked so brown, so ungainly, so rustic. Now they were the right size she could study them better; and they were decidedly shabby, a little eccentric-looking. Mrs Tom's pointed black lace-up shoes which showed beneath her long blue dress were scuffed and old and Mr Tom's jacket was frayed at the cuffs.

'I expect they are tired,' said Marakite following Martha's look. 'It is an effort to bring two of the younger race here by the route you chose. Let's leave them to rest quietly, shall we? In the meanwhile, *do* please go on, Jonathan. Your understanding and grasp of motor-propelled vehicles on Earth is remarkable for a boy of your age, quite remarkable . . . Let's have a little music by way of a break; Martha, you shall choose. Would you like something jolly or something thoughtful? Tell you what, I'll put on quite an easy little thing for you and you can tell me if you like it.'

So saying Marakite rose and made a few adjustments to a table which stood beside his chair: there was a pause: the lighting changed in some subtle way and then the most extraordinary shrieking, whining noise filled the room. It grew in volume, lessened a moment, then was joined by an even more high pitched twang; the two sounds continued together in ever greater head-splitting disharmony.

'Oh, stop it! Please stop it!' called Martha and Jonathan.

'What? You don't like it – oh dear, that *is* a gulf between us.' Marakite switched the music off and stood shaking his head sadly. 'It was so beautiful, you see, so beautiful, so pure, so simple. It was just the music of two crystals split asunder and calling to each other – the first one cries: "Ah come to me my love, life is so long, we must be together in harmony," then the other replies: "Life is long: for true understanding there must be a parting: perhaps we will be as one at the end of all things: when there is fusion and understanding everywhere." The first crystal answers to that – however I see I'm out of your depth. I shall try you with something else presently. After you have slept, perhaps. And then Krita will return and we will introduce you to others in our little community – really we have a very pleasant and cultured group here on the edge of the Great Desert. I can think of so many things to do with you, my dears.'

Jonathan and Martha shifted their position and looked at each other uneasily.

'I wonder what the time is?' said Martha.

'I think we really ought to be getting home soon,' added Jonathan. 'My mother gets awfully bad-tempered if I'm late for meals.'

Marakite looked at them and flung up his hands in amazement. 'But you've only just arrived, you can't possibly think of going yet!' he cried.

'I think we ought to be getting back, all the same,' said Martha as firmly as she could. 'We've been here some time now and we don't want our families worrying about us.'

Marakite had been so polite and nice that she had no doubt that he would accommodate himself to her wish, so it was a little disconcerting when he replied, in his pleasant fluting voice: 'But I shan't let you go, I haven't shown you to *anybody* yet – '

And it was a good deal more disconcerting when Jonathan, in need of support, went to the sofa and shook Mr and Mrs Tom gently, saying, 'Wake up, please, we want to go home,' and they continued to sleep deeply, paying no more attention to him that if he had been a part of their dreams.

'They won't wake.' Jonathan turned to Martha.

'Of course they won't wake,' said Marakite gently. 'Not after the sleeping draught I gave them in their drink. I hope they'll forgive me, but I wanted to have you two delightful children to myself for a while.'

'You mean we can't go?' Martha sprang to her feet, and the full horror of their position came suddenly over her: here they were, trapped on Mars, impossibly far from rescue, and dependent on a man – on a *creature* – who in some ways was totally alien to them, in spite of his fair speech. Why, black might be white in his world and evil good!

Everything might be different, including morals, including keeping guests longer than they wished to stay. Never, never in her whole life had she wanted to return home more than at this precise moment.

'Oh, yes,' said Marakite, smiling, and putting his elbows on his chair arms and his long tapered – too long, too tapered – fingers together and regarding her humorously over them:

'I am going to keep you both for a long, long time. You will be the newest, most delightful sensation our little group has had for a thousand years (our years, not yours, of course). I doubt if you'll return home until you're quite old – human lives go in a flash, don't they? And *don't* worry about not having brought your luggage with you, and little things like that. We can always fit you out with something. Just relax and I'm sure we can make your visit a pleasant one!'

Not to return home until they were quite old! Jonathan and Martha looked at each other in horror. What would their families do without them? What would happen to their families? Perhaps they would never see their parents again: by the time they reached the Earth their parents would be dead.

'You can't do that to us!' cried Jonathan wildly. 'You can't keep us against our will!'

'But my dears, I'm not – you're at perfect liberty to go now if you must – if you know the way back? You need to find just the right hole in the space-time curve if you want your trip to be a quick one – but perhaps you know all about it?'

'Not without Mr and Mrs Tom.' Martha took a turn at shaking them, but with no result, even when she lost her temper and went so far as to slap Mrs Tom on the cheek. Immediately, frightened at having hurt her, she took a pace backwards and said hastily: 'I'm so sorry, Mrs Tom, I didn't mean to hurt you,' but Mrs Tom never woke.

'They must wake sometime,' said Jonathan desperately.

'But you won't be here when they do,' said Marakite. 'There's the whole of Mars to see: I suggest we get started right away. There are the Dead Seas and the Live Seas, the Orange Deserts of sand and of stone, the Great Jewelled Caverns, the Hanging Pillars, the Singing Stones: a thousand wonders, so come, Martha, come Jonathan.'

'No!' cried Martha wildly. She tried to evade Marakite's long fingers and fell back onto the sofa, colliding with Jonathan so that he over-balanced and sat down next to her.

'Perhaps you can stay there a little while?' suggested Marakite. 'While I go and fetch a few of my dear friends whom I am sure would simply love to meet you.'

He walked rapidly away and something behind Jonathan and Martha began to move and writhe, and silvery snake-like things, squirming in a life-like way, only they had no heads, undulated out from the back of the sofa, catching their arms and legs in soft tentacles so that they were fastened down and could not move.

'This is dreadful!' cried Martha, wriggling desperately. 'What shall we do? I don't want to stay on Mars for years and years.'

'Perhaps the wish wouldn't last as long as that,' said Jonathan, but he writhed as much as Martha, and panted with the effort. His face was very white.

There was the sound of voices approaching from the hall. High-pitched and metallic voices, not quite human.

'Wish! Wish!' cried Jonathan, his face contorted as he struggled. 'I wish we were back home!' sobbed Martha, not knowing if this would wake the Toms. But at her words, they jerked and stirred and then the air about them began to move and flicker in a strange way. Martha was just conscious of Marakite approaching them and calling out in a wail of disappointment: 'Oh, if only I'd known! They're Wishing People; I could have taken counter-measures, oh, *botheration*!' and then everything went black. For a few seconds Martha had the sensation that she was travelling upside down in a highly unpleasant fashion – and then she opened her eyes to find herself sprawled uncomfortably on her bedroom carpet. Beside her Jonathan was stirring and rubbing his eyes, and over the floor she saw the doll-like figures of Mr and Mrs Tom rise to their feet, and shake themselves.

'That was rather sudden,' she heard Mr Tom say. 'In fact I'm not altogether sure what happened!'

'Another wish happened,' replied his wife. 'While you were snoring away. A bad failing in duty if I may say so, Mr Tom, to fall asleep in charge of a wish. It has really shaken me up, having to bring us back as swiftly as that, without any warning. Snapping back to the body like that was dangerous for us all. Do you feel all right, children?'

'Yes, I suppose so,' said Martha and Jonathan, getting slowly to their feet. They both felt rather trembly, and very tired.

'We shall need a nice long rest before the last wish,' said Mrs Tom, 'so don't you come bothering us for some days, please. And now you had better go downstairs, I heard somebody calling you.'

'Did you hear what Mrs Tom said?' remarked Jonathan as they shakily picked their way down the stairs. 'We used up two wishes this afternoon. So we have only one more left. One last wish.'

'Don't talk to me about wishes now,' said Martha, shuddering.

'I wonder what we had better have,' continued Jonathan thoughtfully. He paused a moment, then was struck by an absolutely brilliant idea.

'I know what to wish for!' he said, but he spoke to empty air. Martha had gone into the kitchen, from which rather succulent smells were drifting.

So Jonathan went home, to his own supper.

11

It took Martha three days to recover from her trip to Mars.
Some of the time she spent in bed, with a bad cold. She did not
see Jonathan for nearly a week, for by the time she was back at
school, he, in his turn, was away.

When she came back from school on the fourth day after
going to Mars, she was astonished to find Mr and Mrs Tom
busily painting their house with the bright green paint.

'We had no end of trouble levering the top off,' said Mrs
Tom severely to Martha, as if this had been her fault.

'Never mind, it's coming on nicely now,' called Mr Tom
cheerfully from the other side of the house. he was wielding
what was to a man of his size an immensely long paint brush,
and Martha recognized it and the smaller one Mrs Tom was
using as being paint brushes from her own box of paints which
lived somwhere at the bottom of her games cupboard.

'The cupboard door was open and we saw the brushes, and
so we thought we'd get on with the job,' said Mrs Tom.

'But I thought you weren't keen on the colour, or on
smartening the house up,' said Martha in bewilderment.

'Now what can have given you that impression, I wonder?'
Mrs Tom lowered her own brush to survey her husband's
work. 'Careful, Mr T. Your brush is too wet. You're slopping
it all over the place.'

'May I help?' Martha couldn't help feeling that she could
complete the job more easily than they, hampered as they
were by their size.

'You can make a start on the back if you like,' Mrs Tom
told her, rather grudgingly.

So to Martha's surprise, for she had never thought of

spending the evening in this way, she and the Toms painted busily, in companionable silence for the most part, though with the occasional command and criticism from Mrs Tom.

'Not bad,' she said at the end. 'Not bad at all. Though the smell of paint is extremely strong. I suspect it will keep me awake tonight.'

'I think your house looks lovely now,' said Martha, beginning to clean the brushes and clear up. She had enjoyed herself, and it had been nice being with the Toms in a relaxed sort of way, without the strain of magic happenings.

'We've only one wish left,' she said for no particular reason, to Mrs Tom.

'We are well aware of that,' was the reply.

'It's very important, the last wish,' said Martha thoughtfully.

'It could be.' Which of them had answered her? They stood close together, looking up at her, and something in their strained expressions struck her.

'Does it matter to you what we wish?' she asked. 'Does it make a difference?'

'Yes, it does. You see – '

'Hush, my dear,' Mr Tom held his hand over his wife's mouth, preventing her from saying anything else. 'Not allowed.'

'No, you're right,' she bowed her head. There was a silence. Martha looked from one to the other, a little puzzled.

'Anyway, I'm in no hurry,' she told them. 'And it must be Jonathan's wish too. I must wait for him.'

The next day neither she nor the Toms mentioned the subject of wishes, nor the next. The day after that was Saturday.

And on Friday night, or rather in the early hours of Saturday morning, Martha had a dream.

She dreamt she was asleep. She was perfectly aware of her body lying cosy and warm in bed, but she was also in another body which was high in the air somewhere above their house. She was aware that this body could shrink or grow just as she willed it; a little like Alice in Wonderland when she drinks the

126

medicine marked 'Drink me'. Huge, stretching somehow right across the sky, she looked down on the tiny toy-like houses below, each with its sleeping family inside, and immediately beneath her was her own house.

She could see through the roof to her parents in bed in their room, her father snoring slightly, her mother's face buried in the pillow; she could see Anna, flat on her back, her mouth wide open; she could see Paul and Mark in their bunk beds. Mark's blankets were in a tousled heap, half on the floor. Poor things, she thought of her family, pitying them in their blind sleep and unknowingness. And then she half opened her eyes, sleepily, and there on the floor not far from her bed, was the weather house, and she could hear its occupants just beginning to stir and cough.

Suddenly Martha sat up in bed. She was wide awake. Now she had some idea of what her last wish should be, but would Jonathan agree?

'I know exactly what to ask for!' announced Jonathan through their dividing hedge the next morning, where he had spotted Martha playing with Toby in the garden. 'Let me finish cleaning out Hercules and I'll come round and we'll make the wish together.'

'We can't talk about it in front of Mr and Mrs Tom,' said Martha anxiously. 'I'll come round to you.'

'You didn't need to come round,' Jonathan said when she reappeared in his garden. 'It's all so simple. For our last wish we'll just ask for ten more wishes – and so on for ever! We get cleverer and cleverer at it with practice and nothing will ever go wrong!'

'Oh, Jonathan!' said Martha blankly. 'Yes – it *is* a good idea. But – '

She walked about in front of Hercules's run, hardly knowing what she was doing.

'What's the "but" for?' asked Jonathan. 'Whatever you were thinking of for the last wish, you can still have it. Don't you understand? But we must have *my* wish first.'

'Yes, yes, I understand all right,' burst out Martha. 'It's

just if – if we did what I was thinking we should do, we won't have any more wishes at all.'

'That's silly, then.' Jonathan turned from her dismissively to poke a lettuce leaf through the mesh of the run.

'Jonathan, you don't understand,' Martha exclaimed. 'You aren't thinking of the Toms at all: they aren't just magical objects, they're *people*, Jonathan. Seeing them the right size on Mars made me realize it more than ever. And we still don't know enough about them. Before we do anything more I want to talk to them, even if they can't advise us. Come round to my room with me now you've done Hercules and we'll talk to them.'

'All right. But I thought you didn't want to talk about it in front of them.'

'I've changed my mind,' said Martha helplessly.

'All right,' he said again, quite peaceably and reasonably. 'But I can't see what's wrong with my idea.'

They opened Martha's bedroom door and Mr and Mrs Tom instantly appeared at the doors of their shiny new-looking house.

They said nothing but looked so alert and anxious that Martha was strengthened in her resolve.

'The house looks much nicer,' commented Jonathan. He sat himself on the window sill, his legs swinging.

'May I ask you one or two questions?' began Martha carefully. 'I know you can't advise us what to wish for, but you can answer questions, can't you?'

'Ask away,' said Mrs Tom briskly.

'Well firstly I wanted to know – can you ever be released from your enchantment and go back to your proper size in your house wherever it used to be? And does this have something to do with us?'

Mrs Tom's hand shot out and clasped her husband's hand and Martha could see from the whitening of the skin about the knuckles how tightly she held him.

'Yes, I can answer that now you have asked it,' she said very gravely. 'There is one way to release us. And it is up to you and Jonathan.'

128

'Yes, that was what I thought,' said Martha under her breath. Out loud she went on, still carefully thinking it out. 'Now if our last wish was for something like – oh, like a pony (all right Jonathan, I'm not going to wish that) what would happen to you two afterwards?'

'We would grant the wish and then turn back into wooden figures inside our house until the next child found us and began the wishes all over again.'

'That might be never.'

'It certainly might not be for a very long time, but time is a little different for us,' said Mr Tom steadily.

'Suppose we were to wish for another ten wishes and so on, would you be bound to grant them?' put in Jonathan eagerly.

The Toms looked at him and Martha saw a kind of quiver pass over them.

'Yes,' answered Mr Tom in a loud, clear voice. 'This doesn't often come up where Wishing People are concerned because there's usually a clause in the contract to prevent it; otherwise the wishes would go on for ever, or at least until the giver of wishes died of exhaustion, but we didn't make it, for one reason – '

'What reason?' asked Martha and Jonathan together.

'Because don't you see,' broke in Mrs Tom eagerly. 'It gives us another chance. At least the wishes are keeping us alive, not asleep as wooden figures. And though it might kill us we always have the chance that the wisher will eventually tire of his or her demands and make the wish that releases us.'

'So we *can* make a wish that releases you?' pursued Martha cautiously. 'What would you do then?'

'Oh, what would we do? Why, we would return to our house and everything would be as it was. We would have another chance. We would live properly again.'

'Where was your house?' asked Jonathan.

Mr and Mrs Tom looked at one another.

'I think this is where we must tell them more about ourselves Mr T, don't you?' said Mrs Tom. She dropped her husband's hand and seated herself carefully on the step of the weather house.

'I think you must have gathered by now that we are of an older, and altogether superior race of being from yourselves?'

'Not always altogether superior, my dear,' put in Mr Tom gently. 'We have no right to say that now.'

'Well – be that as it may, this is a very imperfect world, as I expect you'd noticed, children. I'm not going to explain how we Wishing People first got here, that is another story altogether, and some of it you wouldn't understand, but we're partly here to help you ordinary Earth people, lighten your burdens, cheer you up a bit, make you see the cracks in what you call "reality". For you can be so sunken in your day to day living you never wake up at all. I flatter myself we've shaken that somewhat, at least. Most of us Wishing People have now moved away to worlds far from Earth, but there are always a very few about the place: it's compulsory, in fact, to do some time here. All of us have great magic powers, though we tend to use them differently. Mr Tom and I had an especial interest in children. We used to grant wishes to them as a present or reward from time to time, not ever as many as ten, but perhaps one or two. They had to be deserving children,' added Mrs Tom, in her best reproving manner. 'And we did various useful jobs about the place, keeping out the forces of evil, bad elementals, that kind of thing. But then we . . . I'm afraid you'll find this difficult to believe, but we began to quarrel.'

'We wanted different things, you see,' Mr Tom explained. 'Mrs Tom scolded me rather; well, as you've noticed perhaps, she liked to have everything just so. And I, I freely admit it, perhaps I grew a little lazy and stubborn to counteract her nagging.'

'And then,' continued Mrs Tom resolutely, 'it's hard to explain how it happened or which of us began it, but we started to do the one thing that Wishing People are expressly forbidden to do.'

'What's that?' asked Martha and Jonathan together.

'We began to give wishes to ourselves. Oh, nothing much at first. Little things to save time. That the fish would rise well when Mr Tom went fishing.'

'More than that,' he said sorrowfully. 'I once wished I could catch a particularly big trout who had always been too cunning for me – and so I did. And when I'd got him I wished I hadn't. It wasn't fair. He looked at me so reproachfully that I put him back.'

'And I wished that my seedlings would always come up and my pastry rise deliciously – and then I began to wish that Mr Tom would come home for his meals on time – '

'And I wished she would stop bothering me,' he put in.

'And then, I shall never forget the day, we were both looking after a wish for a perfectly deserving little boy who had saved some lambs from a savage dog, and we began to quarrel in the middle of the wish and quite forgot it, and it all went wrong.

'There was a terrible thunderstorm with hailstones and a whirlwind lifted up the boy and put him down, quite safely, luckily, in the middle of a haystack half a mile away. Crops were damaged for miles round and trees blown down. Well, though we did our best to make amends it wasn't the sort of thing one can cover up, and so a very high-up overseer indeed came to call on us. We have never felt so ashamed in our lives. The overseer said to us (he was very tall, in a long sweeping robe, and he made us feel so small and contemptible), "Do you realize," he said, "I could not only take away your powers for ever, but I could send your erring souls right back down the ladder of existence into the bodies of animals. How about being sloths in the South American jungle? Or African warthogs? Nice lazy piggy lives for you both, just as you seem to desire! Eventually you might be lucky enough to work your way to being some sort of humans again . . .".'

'We pleaded and pleaded,' Mr Tom took up the tale, 'and at last he said "It is very irregular, but I have a good idea. I fancy there is something neat about it, because I shall tie you to the whims of chance and of children. You may be undone in the process; it may take a hundred years, it may take a thousand. I shall bind you to your house, and to the weather, and to the wishes of children, and the only way to release you will be by the children's own wish." So this is how it happened.'

'And now you know,' said Mrs Tom, obviously making a big

effort to be brisk and brave, her chin up. 'We're in your hands, Martha and Jonathan. We can't say anything further. Mr T, let us take a little turn about the room, while they think about it.'

Jauntily flourishing her umbrella with one hand, Mrs Tom took her husband's arm with the other, and they set off across the floor.

Jonathan and Martha looked at each other.

'I agree that Mr and Mrs Tom should be freed from their enchantment,' said Jonathan in a low voice to Martha, 'but why does it have to be by the next wish? Why not let's have nine more and then release them? I don't see why we shouldn't do that.'

'Oh no, Jonathan; I'm sure we've had enough – they never go quite right – and I think the Toms have had enough too.'

'That's all very well,' said Jonathan stubbornly. 'But you've had one more wish than me. I think I should catch up, anyway.'

'I'm sorry!' cried Martha. 'But I still think it's been enough. If you can't understand, you can't, but I know I'm right.'

'There's no need to shout.'

'I'm not shouting!'

'You are now,' he said irritatingly.

'Oh!' cried Martha, stamping her foot.

'You lose your temper too easily,' said Jonathan icily. 'You can't see what's fair. I need some extra wishes. There are so many things we haven't done. You're just scared of it!'

'I'm not scared! It's just that – well – it was my weather house first of all, wasn't it? It was jolly kind of me to include you. And now I want to be kind to the Toms and you're stopping me!'

'Suppose I wanted to be kind too?' said Jonathan coldly, and with an air of great stubbornness. 'I don't see why I should always do what you want. I wish for ten more – '

'No, I wish – ' Martha shouted just in time. Neither of their wishes could be heard distinctly because their voices drowned each other.

'Stop it! Stop it! Oh, for goodness sake stop it!'

Mr and Mrs Tom had come running back into the centre of the room with looks of great alarm. 'You'll harm us, you could kill us,' cried Mrs Tom, frantically waving her umbrella. 'Never, never wish like that, two of you together! You can't do that with magic, it's far too strong. It'll all get out of control!'

'Look out of the window!' cried Martha suddenly. 'The sky; what's happened to the sky?'

What had been blue sky outside had turned hazy white. Grey streamers of low cloud were blowing past; the trees in the garden tossed about in a sudden, vicious wind, and a door downstairs slammed shut with a crash. The whole house seemed to tremble, and the window panes in Martha's room rattled.

And then something truly dreadful happened. Mrs Tom uttered a loud cry, suddenly spun round, her hand to her chest, dropped her umbrella, and fell to the floor – lifeless.

'Irene, are you all right? What an extraordinary thing to happen! Come in and sit down. Let me give you a cup of tea – or – you're white and shaking – how about a little nip of brandy?'

Martha, entering the kitchen, found her mother hovering solicitously over Jonathan's mother. 'That was the most dreadful gust of wind, I've never seen anything like it,' she exclaimed to Martha. 'It simply got hold of poor Irene while she was hanging out the washing in her garden, and blew her through the gap in the hedge into ours! Here's the brandy, Irene, take a good swig.'

'Thank you,' said Jonathan's mother in a dazed sort of way. She was still clutching a pair of Jonathan's pants. 'I don't think I'm hurt really, just a few scratches.'

'You sit there and recover,' said Mrs Grant sympathetically. 'Martha – '

But Martha had gone, plus the bottle of brandy.

She ran upstairs with it, her heart pounding. Mrs Tom still lay, a small pathetic figure, stretched on her bedroom floor, but Martha was relieved to see that she was now moving slightly. Her head was cradled on her husband's lap.

'Brandy?' he said again, as he had cried out a few minutes previously. 'Have you any brandy?'

'Here it is,' cried Martha, pouring a little into a doll's teacup which stood with a few other pieces of china on her chest of drawers. She was greatly relieved to see Mrs Tom drink a little, cough, sneeze, and then sit up.

'What happened?' she asked.

'You fainted, my dear. Thank goodness it was nothing more than that. The ill effects are passing, the wind's dying. But it was a near thing. Upon my word, I think I'll have a taste of that brandy too.'

'You're not to take too much, it doesn't agree with you,' said Mrs Tom, obviously much better, and scrambling to her feet. 'I'm all right now.'

'I'm terribly sorry,' cried Jonathan. 'I didn't mean that to happen. Was it because I was so set on my extra wishes? I don't know what came over me. I just felt I *must* have them. But now I feel quite different.'

'You mean you agree to give Mr and Mrs Tom their freedom for the last wish?' said Martha eagerly.

'Yes. It's too dangerous to go on. I see that now. I might not ever have wanted to stop. I'd always have wanted one more.'

'Yes! Yes!' cried Mr Tom eagerly. 'That's precisely it. One gets a taste for magic; it gets a hold of you. It had the beginnings of one on you, Jonathan, until you were shocked out of it.'

'You're not bad children, though full of faults and very ignorant,' put in Mrs Tom. 'But I think your hearts are in the right place. If you'd gone on and on the desire to have one perfect last wish and solve all your problems, would have grown and grown until, poof, suddenly one, or both, of us were dead. The toy would have been broken. And it wouldn't have done you any good, either.'

'I see that now,' said Jonathan thoughtfully. 'But my wishes weren't all going to be for me. In a way the one I'm sorriest about not having was one for my mum. I wanted to wish that she'd make some friends. She's always going on about being lonely here, and I'm frightened she'll make us move away.

Somehow she's never got on with your mum, has she, Martha?'

'She is now!' said Martha eagerly, remembering the scene downstairs. 'She's boozing brandy like anything and they're both talking away. I'll bet they like each other more after this. My mum loves people when they're not well or in trouble.'

'It's an ill wind,' said Mrs Tom reflectively. 'And I feel quite recovered now, so, how about it, Martha, how about it?'

'Yes, let's make the last wish. Tell me exactly what to say.'

'Wait!' cried Mrs Tom. 'Not so fast. We'll do this properly.' She pulled her little notebook out of her pocket, her hands trembling with excitement so that she almost dropped it.

'It must be entered and signed for, just like the others,' she said. 'And we won't make it here. Take us out to beyond the beechwoods, near the place where you had your first wish, and then we'll show you something, and say goodbye to you there. Don't you agree, Mr Tom?'

'You are right, as always, my dear,' he said, and leaning forward he kissed her lightly on the cheek.

'Spoony old thing,' remarked Mrs Tom, her lips trembling as if she were repressing a smile of pleasure. 'Just you keep your lips to yourself.'

But the look she gave Mr Tom was very amiable.

'The sun's shining again,' said Jonathan, leaning out of the window. 'And the birds are singing away like anything. It's as if it was the beginning of another day.'

12

'A picnic for the two of you?' called Martha's mother rather vaguely from the sitting room, where she was now drinking coffee with Jonathan's mother. 'Why not? That awful wind seems to have quite died down. You'll have to forage for yourselves in the kitchen; at least I've plenty of bread. Is their going off for the afternoon all right by you, Irene?'

'Fine, fine, have a good time!' called Jonathan's mother in a bright, happy voice which was so different from her normal one that Martha hardly recognized it.

Hastily Martha and Jonathan threw some food into a carrier bag, put the weather house into another and ran out of the front gate, where they met Toby, returning from one of his expeditions looking muddy and disreputable, with one ear turned rakishly inside out, showing the pink lining. Immediately he saw them and smelled the picnic he wanted to join them, jumping about them gleefully.

'Oh no, Toby, you can't,' exclaimed Martha in horror, remembering what had happened the last time he had come too close to the Toms.

She dragged the reluctant dog back into the house and shut the door on him.

'Quick!' she said, and so she and Jonathan set off as rapidly as they could up the road towards the hills.

They couldn't keep up the pace for long, it was growing too hot, and soon they settled to a steady walk, turning at last thankfully up the white chalky track that wound up into the beechwoods.

It had become a brilliant day. The sky stretched overhead, glittering blue, vivid green barley fields gave way to equally green pasture dotted with white sheep, the white stones of the track hurt the eyes and it was a relief to enter the hushed, cool woods, where the mossy path was soft and kind to their feet and the sun fell only in little trembling pools of light. Here they paused awhile and had their picnic. Mr and Mrs Tom climbed out of their weather house and sat on its roof and when the picnic was over Martha carried them carefully on again, while they directed her.

'Take the left hand path and don't jog us so,' and then, 'Now right, by that fallen tree trunk, and out onto the grass beyond it.'

They obeyed the directions and found themselves on the edge of the wood, in a grassy clearing about fifty yards from the summit of the hill.

'Oh, I'd like to live here!' cried Martha enthusiastically. 'Aren't the wild flowers gorgeous, Jonathan? Look, there's loads of thyme and mint and speedwell and harebells – and what's the yellow flower? And those white ones?'

'Come on, Martha, less fussing about among the flowers! How about putting us down and placing our house for us?' cried Mrs Tom, and so they did so and the Toms stood before it, directing the siting of it to an exact spot on a great carpet of blue speedwell, and suddenly it struck Martha that of course it was going to be the very best site of all for a house; for the Tom's house.

'Now, Martha, you may say your last wish,' cried Mrs Tom, and Martha stammered, aware of the solemnity of the occasion – ' – I don't know how best to say it. You say it for me, Mrs Tom.'

'Tch, tch,' said Mrs Tom briskly. 'There's nothing specially difficult to it. Repeat after me then, slowly and clearly . . . Wait. I've written it down, to finish the record. Here it is in my little book. Repeat after me then: "My last wish is that Mr and Mrs Tom be released from their bondage to return to their house for ever; having completed their task to my complete satisfaction." I'm putting it solely in your mouth, you see, Martha,' she said, 'because you are in fact the prime wisher, and the one who found us, important though it was that you and Jonathan should be in agreement over this wish. So – ' Mrs Tom took a deep breath – 'Ready, Martha? Ready, Mr T?'

Martha had opened her mouth, was just beginning on the wish when Mr Tom suddenly shouted:

'Hold!' in a loud, ringing voice.

They all paused and looked at him as he strode, a small yet impressive figure, to the weather house and stood, his arms out to bar the entrances.

'Stop!' he said again.

'My dear man, have you taken leave of your senses?'

Mrs Tom went up to him and put her hand on his arm, but he shook her away.

'No; you must listen to me now. Before things return to as they were before, we must come to an agreement, you know we must, or I'm not coming with you!'

'Not coming with me!'

Mrs Tom, looking very bewildered, stepped back a pace and stood so still that a wandering ladybird, who had been inspecting her left shoe with great interest (it was nearly the same size as it was itself) decided it was a good place to sit on. Mrs Tom did not even notice it.

'You must give me your word finally and forever,' said Mr Tom, looking as stern and determined as Martha had ever seen him, 'that although we return to our house for a period of time, for two hundred years, for three hundred years, one day we leave it and we go on, as so many of the others have done. We leave the hills, for these *are* only the hills, and we go on to the mountains. Nothing that can change and grow is for ever and we must progress. You will accept that now?'

Mrs Tom looked about her, suddenly seeing the ladybird and prodding it off her shoe with the point of her umbrella. 'Fly away, silly thing,' she said. Then, ' – Oh, all right, all right. My lovely house, all my things, my garden – yes, I'll do as you say, when you say. I give you my word and I'm an honourable woman, as I've mentioned before, I think. And now, Martha, speak the wish.'

She went to stand by her husband and Martha spoke the

wish and gradually, gradually they saw the air begin to
shimmer about the weather house and it grew and grew and
Mr and Mrs Tom grew with it. The two doors became one
door with a window on either side; a porch with clematis and
roses climbing over it appeared in front of the door and there
stood a charming green and white wooden house before them,
just inviting them to step inside.

Mr and Mrs Tom stretched out their arms and looked at
one another and smiled; ordinary, normal sized people. Mrs
Tom about five foot one, and Mr Tom about five foot seven.
They were the same height they had been on the trip to Mars.

'Thank goodness I'm a proper size again!' cried Mrs Tom.
'You've no idea, children, how beastly it was to be so small.'

As for Mr Tom, he smiled and smiled and shook Martha
and Jonathan by the hand as if he would never leave off.

'Can we come in and see round your house?' Martha asked
eagerly.

But the Toms shook their heads regretfully, and went to
stand barring the threshold.

'Not if you want to keep living in your present bodies,' said
Mrs Tom. 'And I would advise you to keep to them for some
time yet now, having got them. Time is different in our house:
returning to it we will inhabit the world on a different level
from yours. It is only by a strong effort of will on our side that
you can see us and the outside of the house at all now. Soon we
will have to give up the illusion and leave you.'

'But we wanted to say thank you so very much,' put in Mr
Tom, bowing to them with a flourish of his hat. 'We are
deeply obliged to you both.'

'Yes, we are indeed. I hate goodbyes, but goodbye it is.
You're not bad children. You'll do all right, I daresay. As I
said, I can't stand goodbyes. I'm going indoors to put the
kettle on for a nice cup of tea. I'm absolutely longing for it.'

And with an odd little nod and a sniff Mrs Tom opened the
door and disappeared inside. Mr Tom continued to stand in
the porch, but something strange was beginning to happen to
the air all about him. It shook as if it were a great, nearly
invisible curtain; it shimmered and vibrated. There was a low

humming sound. It was impossible to see past Mr Tom into the house and even he, standing in the porch as he was, his hat in his hand, was becoming difficult to see very clearly.

Instinctively Martha and Jonathan retreated a few paces, away from the shimmering air.

'Goodbye! Goodbye!' came Mr Tom's voice and he waved and waved his hat. 'Goodbye my dears, goodbye!'

'Goodbye! shouted Martha and Jonathan together.

'Aren't we ever going to see you again?' cried Martha then, suddenly realizing her loss; how she would miss them, not only for the magic but for their company and friendship. It had ended so quickly, how could she manage without them? She had a moment of wild regret for all the unknown magic she would never experience again. Through the humming, dazzling light which surrounded the cottage, she saw Mr Tom shake his head.

'Goodbye, goodbye!' he continued to call. And now it seemed as if great white waves fell crashing soundlessly between them: the house tilted sideways: there was an unforgettable glimpse past it of the hills beyond: the same hills, and yet in some impossible-to-describe way not the same hills, and all bathed in white light – and then nothing.

The house had gone, the gap closed; nothing was left except the echo of a calling voice, 'Goodbye!'

Soon that had gone too and there was just a faint sound of a breeze stirring the leaves of the trees behind them and of dozens of larks high over the grassy slopes ahead.

Jonathan and Martha found they were sitting on the carpet of blue speedwell close together. Feeling strangely stiff and dazed, as if more time had gone by than they had realized, they got slowly to their feet, tears running down both their faces.

'I wish we'd wished to see them again,' said Martha, mournfully.

'I wish we'd had a wish that had lasted,' said Jonathan. 'Something to show for it all. We didn't think enough about our wishes. We thought we were thinking but we weren't.'

'If we'd had a year to think between every wish I wonder if we'd ever have thought of the very best wish to have, whatever it was,' agreed Martha.

'Is there *anything* that works out the very way one wants it to?' said Jonathan a little bitterly.

'We didn't know what we truly wanted, I suppose.'

'Flying was good.'

'Yes – and we'll never do it again. Except in our dreams.'

'One can't have good dreams whenever one wants to. And we could have nightmares. I'm sure I'll have one about Mars sometime.'

'Probably you won't, now you've talked about it,' said Martha, cheering up a little. 'It's things one never thinks of one has nightmares about. Haven't you found that?'

'I don't know,' replied Jonathan doubtfully. 'Come to think of it I don't believe I've ever had a nightmare in the whole of my life.'

They walked thoughtfully on, into the shade of the beech-woods. Both felt not only a sadness at saying goodbye to the Toms, but a feeling of frustration, as if something truly important had eluded them; something they were just about to grasp, to understand.

There were places where the trees clustered less densely, and there the light pierced through, in patches and little pools of colour. The sun, glinting down, picked out something moving, a small, busy, white shape, running hither and thither, its nose to the ground.

'Toby!' cried Martha in amazement.

She whistled to him and he instantly ran to them, frisking about them and jumping up and trying to lick their faces.

'Imagine it,' said Martha proudly to Jonathan. 'He must have got out and tracked us all the way here. It's a long way. He's never done anything so good before.'

'You're a very clever dog, Toby,' said Jonathan solemnly, patting him. Toby wagged his tail, as if quite in agreement, delighted to have found them.

And so they went back through the woods; boy, girl, dog;

and out on to the chalky track that led the way home, into the warm golden light and all the insect-and-bird-filled hum and chatter of a fine summer's afternoon.

Soon they began to feel much better.